Bring on The Night

Autumn and Matt
Love in Nashville Book One

By SJ McCoy

A Sweet n Steamy Romance

Published by Xenion, Inc

Published by Xenion, Inc.
First paperback edition 2019
www.sjmccoy.com

This book is a work of fiction. Names, characters, places, and events
are figments of the author's imagination, fictitious, or are used
fictitiously. Any resemblance to actual events, locales or persons
living or dead is coincidental.

Cover Design by Dana Lamothe of Designs by Dana
Editor: Mitzi Pummer Carroll
Proofreaders: Aileen Blomberg, Marisa Nichols, Traci Atkinson.

ISBN 978-1-946220-53-0

Dedication

For Sam. Sometimes, life really is too short. Few x

Chapter One

Summer hugged Autumn tight, and Autumn made a face at Carter over her shoulder.

"It's been so wonderful to see you. I wish you'd come up here more often."

"You know I come when I can," Autumn said. "And besides, you could always come and see me."

Summer smiled. "It isn't as easy for us. Not with the baby and everything."

"That's why I get here as often as I can."

"I know. I'm not complaining; it's just that I miss you so much," Summer said with a sad smile.

"I miss you, too, sis. I'll figure out when I can get back up here soon." Autumn turned and smiled at Carter. "It was good to see you, too, big guy."

Carter gave her that bashful smile of his. He was such a good guy, and Autumn was glad that Summer had found him. They were so happy together, and although the life they'd made up here in Montana wouldn't suit her, she could see that it was ideal for them.

"It was great to see you. And you know that I'm with Summer; I hope you can get back up again soon. Even though

I know it's not fair that the onus is on you to come here. Maybe one of these weekends we'll ask my parents to have Penny, and we'll come down to Nashville to visit you."

Autumn grinned at him. "You really are the sweetest guy on earth, aren't you? I know how much the idea of coming to Nashville appeals to you. I know you'd rather go have a tooth pulled than spend a weekend in the city."

He gave her his bashful grin again. "I'm not going to lie. It's not my idea of fun, but you know how important family is to me, and you're family. And besides, you shouldn't have to be the one doing all the running."

Autumn smiled at him. "I don't mind. I should go."

Summer laughed. "Okay, I know how good you are at long goodbyes. We'll head out and leave you to it."

Carter frowned. "I know it's nearly time, but I hate to leave you here to wait by yourself."

Autumn laughed. "You're hardly leaving me at the bus station. This is a private airport. The jet guys will be here soon."

"If you're sure." Carter still didn't look happy.

"She is." Summer gave her a knowing smile. "She just wants us to go now."

"Thanks again, guys." Autumn hugged them both and then stepped back. "I know you're both better at goodbyes than I am, but I just want to get out of here." She shrugged at Summer. "You know I always need a little transition time. I need to shut down the me that I've been with you guys and get my work head back on."

Carter raised an eyebrow at that. But she knew that Summer understood.

"It's true." Summer smiled at her husband. "We're lucky that she's prepared to be her relaxed and happy self with us. I don't think you'd deal too well with the work version of Autumn."

Carter nodded. "We all need a hard, outer shell to deal with the working world sometimes, right, Autumn?"

Autumn laughed. "I sure as hell do, especially considering the people I work with."

Summer gave her a hard stare. "Speaking of the people you work with, how's Matt?"

Autumn returned the stare. "Okay, I'm going to use that as my cue to leave. Just hearing that asshole's name has shaken me out of my warm and fuzzy relaxed self and sets me back into work bitch mode." She picked up her bag and started to walk away.

Summer laughed as she made her retreat. "One day, you're going to have to admit that you like him."

"Whatever you say, little sis. As far as I'm concerned, hell will freeze over before that day ever comes," Autumn called over her shoulder. She turned back when she reached the automatic doors and smiled at the sight of them still standing there watching her. They were such a perfect couple. Summer was so dainty and so pretty, she made Carter look even bigger than he was. If she didn't know them, she might assume that he was a bodyguard rather than her husband. Actually, that wasn't true. Everything about him, every move he made, showed just how much he loved her. Autumn was truly happy for them.

They waved, and Summer blew her a kiss. She blew one back and then turned and went through the doors as fast as she could. Carter didn't know how close he'd been to the truth when he'd talked about her needing a hard shell for work. Without it, she felt too soft – but no, there were no tears pricking behind her eyes because she was leaving.

She hadn't been joking about needing transition time either. She'd told them that the jet would be here to collect her at four o'clock. The truth was, the pilots had called her to tell her that they should be landing around four-thirty.

She made her way over to the sofas in front of the big windows that overlooked the runway. Once she'd made herself and her bag comfortable, she pulled out her phone and checked the flight tracker app. She wasn't surprised to see that they were scheduled to land right on time.

She blew out a sigh. The other thing she hadn't told Summer and Carter was that Matt was on the plane. He'd been in Seattle for the weekend while she was here. She was convinced he'd only gone so that they could fly back to Nashville together. At first, he'd joked about tagging along with her for the weekend, but there was no way she was going to let him do that. The man was a pain in her ass.

Her job as head of McAdam Records meant that she had to work closely with him—considering that he was one of the label's biggest stars. And she worked all the hours that God sent, so Matt was a constant, infuriating presence in her life.

As if to prove her point, her phone buzzed with an incoming text. She shook her head when she saw Matt's name appear on the display. How the hell was he texting when they were still in the air? She scowled. He'd better be on that damned plane. She wasn't relishing the thought of spending the next few hours cooped up in the jet with him, but even that was preferable to figuring out how to get him back to Nashville if he wasn't on it. She opened the text, dreading what she might be about to read.

> *Hey baby girl! Can't wait to see you!*
> *Hope you don't mind I asked the guys to get you first.*
> *I'll see you in Seattle :-)*

Autumn blew out a sigh of sheer aggravation. He had a nerve! What in the hell did he think he was playing at? It would take them a good few hours to get back to Nashville from here. If she first had to fly to Seattle, she probably wouldn't be home before midnight. She scowled as she tapped out a reply

I do mind!
What are you playing at?
You're supposed to be on the damned plane.
I should just go on home without you.

She rolled her eyes when her phone rang, and his name popped up on the screen. He was no doubt going to try to sweet-talk her. Any other man on earth would have taken the hint by now that she just wasn't interested.

"What?!" she answered.

"Hey, baby girl!"

"Don't you baby girl me! What in hell's name do you think you're playing at? You're supposed to be on the plane. We're supposed to be going straight back to Nashville."

"I know, I know. But there's a lot going on here, and I thought you'd enjoy a night in the Emerald City."

"A night?! What are you talking about? It's bad enough that I'm going to have to come there to get you before I go back to Nashville. There's no way I'm spending the night."

"But we'll have so much fun. You work too hard. Come on, when was the last time you just kicked back and let your hair down?"

"All freaking weekend! That's what I came here to Montana for. Now I'm ready to go home and get back to work, and so should you be."

"Don't be mad at me. It'll be fun, you'll see."

"You are out of your freaking mind! I'm not spending the night in Seattle. You'd better be ready when the plane touches down. I'm not even going to get off. You'd better hustle your ass out of the airport and on to the plane. Don't give me a reason to really lose my temper with you."

"Or else what?"

Autumn gritted her teeth. The man was infuriating. She could hear the smile in his voice. He thought he was being cute—or something. Whenever she got mad at him, he thought he could win her over. Why hadn't he learned in all the years that they'd been working together that all he did was piss her off, big time! "You aren't going to find out *or else what*, because you are going to be ready to leave when the plane touches down."

"No, I'm not." He sounded a little less full of himself now.

"Why not? Is there a problem?"

"Not a problem … So much as …"

"Oh, for God's sake, Matt! Can you just tell me what's going on, please?"

"It's a good thing, really. You won't be so mad at me when you understand."

"I'll be the judge of how mad I'm going to be and how good or bad I think it is—if you ever tell me just *what* it is. Come on, spit it out. What the hell is going on?"

"Well, you know how Reggie has been talking about going home?"

"Yes." Autumn frowned. Matt was contracted as a solo artist, but his band had been with him for a long time. The drummer, Reggie, was a few years older than the other guys. He'd left his wife and two little kids at home in Alabama to go on the road for Matt's first big tour a few years ago. He was always taking off for a few days whenever he could to go and see them. Recently, he'd been talking about throwing in the towel and going home to them.

"Well, this weekend he decided to do more than just talk about it. He texted me yesterday to say that he left. He's home in Alabama, and he's not coming back."

"Awesome!" Autumn got to her feet and started to pace. Her mind was racing. "That's all the more reason you need to be ready when I get there. We need to haul ass back to Nashville, and in the morning, we need to bring in all the drummers we know and start auditioning so that we can replace him."

"There's no need. That's what I'm trying to tell you. I knew you wouldn't be happy, so I fixed it myself. Do you remember Weston? He used to work with Shawnee, but he ..."

"Of course, I remember him! He's amazing. But he took off, went to work in Central America, Panama or somewhere."

"That's right. And if you'd let me finish, what I was about to tell you is that I've been in touch with him for a little while, and he's on his way back to the States. In fact, his plane lands at ten o'clock tonight here in Seattle. I figured we could kill two birds with one stone. If we stay here, we can meet with him in the morning."

Autumn blew out a sigh. She could see the logic of it, even if she didn't want to. Trying to find a new drummer in Nashville would take up far too much of both their time this week. Weston was one of the best, not only in terms of talent, but also, he was a great guy with a great work ethic.

She could hear the smirk in Matt's voice when he spoke again. "So, what do you say, baby girl? Want to spend the night with me in Seattle?"

She wanted to say no. Wanted to tell Matt to bring Weston to Nashville, and they could work out the details there. But she was pragmatic if nothing else. She was already on her way to Seattle. Matt was already there. They may as well take care of business. "I'll meet with West with you in the morning. Just tell me when and where. And make it as early as you can. I'm going to have to rearrange my morning schedule; I don't want to have to rearrange my afternoon, too. Text me when you have the meeting set up. I need to go. I'm going to have to find myself a hotel room."

"Aww, don't be like that. Don't dismiss me like I'm just some pain in the ass."

"You're not just *some* pain in the ass. You're the biggest pain in the ass I ever met!"

He chuckled. "Well, at least I made an impression. I'm special. You just admitted it."

Autumn pursed her lips to try to keep in her smile. He was infuriating, but he usually managed to wear her down and make her smile.

"And besides, I knew you'd be mad at me, so I already booked you a room."

She was torn between feeling grateful that he'd taken care of that detail and feeling angry that he was so presumptuous that he knew in advance that she would fall in with his plans.

"You're not going to bite my head off?"

She sighed. "No. There's no point. I'm still mad at you. But ..."

"But you can't stay mad at your best friend, especially when he's about to buy you dinner, right?"

"You're not ..." Autumn began, but then she stopped herself. Could she really deny either of his statements? If he wanted to buy her dinner, she may as well let him. They both had to eat. And as for him being her best friend, well, he might be. She chewed the inside of her lip as she mulled that one over. She didn't really have time for friends. At least, not people who weren't already part of her working world. She probably spent more time with him than with anyone else. He was a royal pain in the ass, but she had to admit that he was a good guy.

The line was quiet for a few moments while he waited for her to continue. She didn't.

"I'm not what?' he asked eventually.

She sighed.

"Okay, I'll take your silence as agreement." The smile was back in his voice. "Of course, I'm about to buy you dinner, and we both know I'm your best friend."

"So, you're meeting me when the plane lands?"

"You betcha. There's this great little Vietnamese place …"

"Yeah. I'll see it when I get there. I need to start rearranging my morning. You'd better have an iced caramel macchiato waiting for me when I land."

"You got it, boss lady."

Autumn set her phone down in her lap and stared out at the mountains for a few moments. This was the way it went. Plans changed. Schedules got rearranged. It made for an interesting life.

Chapter Two

Matt grinned as he hung up. He hadn't expected it to go so well. It seemed that Autumn got mad at him every time they spoke for one reason or another. She just needed to loosen up some. People told him that he should give it up, that she'd never be interested in him, but he knew she was.

He went to stand in front of the wall of windows to look out at the amazing view. He loved Seattle. He loved everything about the place and most especially the view of the water. He loved watching the ferries coming and going to the islands. He didn't even have anyone here to visit anymore. His buddy who used to live here had moved to Oregon last year. But Matt still liked to come and hang out. Just to take in the atmosphere and the cool vibe of the city.

When Autumn had announced that she was going to visit Carter and Summer in Montana this weekend, he decided to hitch a ride in the jet and come on up here. He would rather have gone with her. He and Summer were old buddies, and he knew and liked Carter and his brothers, especially Chance. He'd joked with Autumn that he should go with her, but she'd blown him out of the water as usual.

He checked his watch; she wouldn't be here for a few hours yet. The guys wouldn't even land in Montana for another fifteen minutes or so. Then they'd have to refuel before turning around to come back here. He'd told Clay what he planned to do this evening. He'd offered to pay for the jet fuel since he was adding an unnecessary expense. Of course, Clay had laughed him off. He'd wished him luck as he usually did whenever they spoke about Autumn. In fact, it had been Clay's suggestion that Matt should book a room for her. Matt smirked to himself. If it were down to him, she'd be staying in his room.

He rechecked his watch; he still had plenty of time to kill before he needed to get to the airport to meet her. He smiled and picked up his wallet from the counter. He'd managed to book the room next to his for her. He may as well go out and get a few things that might put him on her good side—or at least, get him off her shit list.

He wandered down by the market. Maybe, hopefully, she'd come walk down here with him later. But he couldn't bank on her saying yes to that, or to anything for that matter, so he bought some coffee and some doughnuts. He knew she loved them both, and finding them waiting in her room might help put her in a better mood.

Zack, one of the pilots, texted him to let him know that they'd landed in Bozeman. They were refueling and planned to take off again as soon as they could. That should put them back on the ground at Boeing Field around 7 p.m.

He walked through the market and out on the terrace overlooking the water. It was still busy, crowded with people enjoying the last of their weekend. He smiled at a little girl who stared up at him as she walked by, holding tightly to her daddy's hand. She was as cute as a button. She stuck her tongue out at him, and he made a face back at her. Her mom caught the interaction and gave Matt a wary look. He felt bad. This wasn't the small-town Georgia he'd grown up in a couple of decades ago. This was the big city, and he should know better. Parents had to look out for their kids these days—they had to be wary of strangers. He gave the woman a smile that he hoped was both apologetic and reassuring at the same time.

It didn't seem to work; she continued to stare at him. Her brows knit together, and Matt waited, wondering what was coming. A wave of relief washed over him when her eyes opened wide in surprise, and she grinned. She'd recognized him. Normally, he wasn't thrilled when that happened, but in this case, he welcomed it.

The woman tapped her husband's arm, and they both stared at him. He lifted his hand in a half wave, hoping that would be the end of it.

No such luck.

The guy came toward him, looking around furtively as if he'd discovered some hidden treasure that he didn't want to share with any of the passersby.

"Are you … you're Matt McConnell, aren't you?"

Matt mirrored his actions, looking around before he answered. Hoping to convey the message that he'd rather not make his identity public. He nodded and gave the guy a conspiratorial smile. "You got me. I was doing so well, too. I managed to go almost a whole day out without being recognized. It was awesome, but I guess the game's up now."

The guy shook his head rapidly and looked around again. "No worries. We won't give you away." He smiled at his wife, and she stepped closer. The little girl smiled up at Matt.

"Seriously?" Matt hoped he sounded surprised and grateful, though he felt kind of bad. He'd pulled this one dozens if not hundreds of times. Sometimes it worked and the people who spotted him kept quiet; sometimes it didn't, and he ended up surrounded by an inquisitive crowd. He felt bad because it only worked on decent people, people who could appreciate his desire to remain anonymous. He didn't like to manipulate good people—but it was preferable to becoming the center of attention and ruining his downtime.

The woman smiled at him. "Of course! Gosh, it must be awful when people recognize you." She looked around as if the other people in the market might suddenly turn zombie and try to eat them. "People can be so awful."

Matt nodded gratefully. "They can, but some can be amazing—like you guys. Thanks so much." He smiled down at the little girl again, and she waved up at him.

"Would you mind if I took your picture with her?" asked the woman.

"Sure." If they wanted to use the kid as their excuse to snap a picture, he wasn't going to say no.

The woman scooped the kid up and stood beside him, and the dad pulled out his cell phone and snapped away, then he leaned in and got a group selfie. Matt smiled and hammed it up for the camera. He didn't mind; in fact, he enjoyed this kind of stuff with fans. It was only when a couple of people turned into a curious mob that it became a problem.

The guy put his phone away and shook his hand. "Thanks, and don't worry, I won't share them on social media or anything. They'll be just for us."

Matt grinned at him. "It's not a problem if you want to post them. I don't mind being seen in photos afterward; I'll be home by the time anyone sees them. If people want to crowd around and ask questions, they'll be asking you. I won't have to deal with it."

The guy smiled back at him. "You really don't mind? We can say we met you?"

Matt nodded. "I don't mind one bit. You can tag me, too. I enjoy all the social stuff." He looked around. "I just don't enjoy being forced to be social with a whole bunch of people on my downtime."

The woman reached out and touch his arm. "We didn't mean to intrude."

He shook his head. "It's fine. Meeting you guys has been fun." He looked around. "It's always cool to make new friends. It's walking the line between making three new friends and attracting three dozen curious pairs of eyes that gets difficult. And on that note, I should scoot."

The little girl tugged on his sleeve. "One more photo?"

He looked at her parents, who nodded eagerly. He scooped her up, and she wrapped her arms around his neck. His smile was genuine as her parents both pulled out their phones and snapped away. Before he set her down again, she landed a sloppy wet kiss on his cheek, making him laugh.

He was still smiling to himself by the time he made it back to his room. The kid was cute, and her parents had been the kind of people he didn't mind bumping into. They were starstruck but reserved enough that they tried not to let it show. He'd have to look out for the photos—he knew they'd show up online somewhere, and he'd be tagged. He wanted to make sure that he commented and said how great it'd been to meet them. It'd only take two minutes of his time, but it'd mean a lot to them. He'd never felt that kind of celebrity fascination himself. He didn't get why people thought that the ability to sing a song or act on TV or in movies made people different—more interesting, somehow—than people who worked in other professions. He didn't get it, but he accepted that it was a thing, and he tried to respect it—for the fans' sake and his own.

He went to stand in front of the wall of windows to look out at the water. He had an amazing view from his apartment in Nashville; he could see most of the city, but it wasn't like this. Here he could see the waterfront and the harbor. He loved the feeling that there was more than just the city. The ferries came and went, bringing people to work and taking them away again—away across the water, back to the peninsula and the islands, to the quieter life. He shook his head. It wasn't as though he craved a quieter life or anything. He'd grown up in the country—it didn't get much quieter than his podunk hometown in Georgia. No, he didn't miss it. Well, he did maybe a little. He didn't want to go back; he just didn't want to forget that it was out there. He'd seen too many people arrive in Nashville with big dreams. Most of them forgot where they came from—whether they made it big or not. They got swallowed up in what it took to survive in the city, in the industry. He didn't want to go down that road. As long as he remembered where he came from and remembered that people were still out there living that life, he couldn't get too caught up in his new life and everything that came with it. The money, the fame, he gave a little shrug; the women, they were all great, but they weren't real. He did his best to make sure that he never forgot that.

He went back to the counter where he'd set down his haul from his little shopping trip. He picked the bags up with a smile and went next door to Autumn's room. He didn't like to stay in hotels when he came to Seattle. He'd discovered this place the first time he came to visit his old buddy, and it had immediately become a favorite. It was a serviced apartment building, mostly inhabited by young corporate types with a few vacationers sprinkled in. He'd gotten to know the leasing agent who lined his own pockets with short-term rentals to the likes of Matt, and who always managed to find him one of the nicer rooms whenever he came to town. He'd been happy to oblige when Matt had called him earlier and asked if there was another apartment free for tonight.

Matt looked around when he let himself in. He hoped Autumn would like it. He couldn't see any reason why she wouldn't. It was just like his; even the décor was the same. He let out a little chuckle. But just because he liked it, that didn't mean anything. Autumn rarely seemed to like the same things he did. He wasn't worried that it wouldn't be up to her standard. She wasn't one of those picky women who demanded perfection. He frowned, well, she did in some things—maybe most things—but she wasn't a pampered princess who needed luxurious accommodation. As long as things were run efficiently, she was happy. She was demanding, if he was honest. But he didn't see her as demanding in a difficult way—though she could be difficult, too. He chuckled again. Maybe she really was difficult and demanding, and he just couldn't see it because she had his head turned so far around? No. That wasn't it. She wouldn't turn his head if she were like that. She was great at what she did. If she was demanding, it was because she demanded excellence—but she demanded it of herself first. She was just so good at whatever she set her mind to, and she expected the same of the people around her.

He set the bag of freshly ground beans next to the coffee pot and the box of doughnuts next to it. Then he went through the cupboards looking for something he could use as a vase. He was pleased when he found an actual vase and filled it with water before arranging the tulips in it. Autumn loved tulips. She liked to make out that she was such a tough nut, but over the years that they'd worked together, Matt had picked up on many of her little idiosyncrasies, and most of them gave her away as a much softer, gentler soul than she presented to the world. She came across as tough—some might even say abrasive, but Matt knew that it was just the way she brought the best out of people—got the result that the label needed. He'd seen her gently coax the younger artists when they needed it. It wasn't so much that she was tough as that she was smart. Her end goal was always to get the best out of people and with most people that meant she had to be tough. She acted like a fairy godmother to Marvin, the janitor at the McAdam building—but then Marvin was one of those guys who loved his job and gave it his all every day. Some folks might look down on the guy who cleaned the restrooms—but Marvin was proud of how those restrooms gleamed. And Autumn appreciated that about him.

Matt set the vase of tulips down on the coffee table and stepped back to admire his work. He was no flower arranger, but they looked good, and hopefully Autumn would appreciate the effort. She didn't usually appreciate his efforts—at anything. He pursed his lips at the thought. Why was that? He worked hard. He put his best into everything he did. So, why did she treat him as if he were something that had stuck to her shoe? He shrugged. Maybe it was because she knew he didn't need her support? He stood on his own two feet, owned his failings as well as his successes. Nah, that wasn't it either. Autumn wasn't about helping weaklings; it was just that she appreciated a job well done. He did his job well—he was great at it if he did say so himself—so why didn't she appreciate him? He sat down on the sofa and stared at the tulips. In the early days, before she took the job as head of McAdam Records, he'd thought that he and Autumn were a sure thing. It was obvious—or so he'd thought—that they were made for each other.

She'd been prickly with him when she was brought in to manage his first big tour. He'd thought she was overdoing the professional distance thing. She couldn't get involved with him; he was her artist. It made sense. And, of course, he'd had that whole shitshow with Sheena Reynolds. He rolled his eyes at the memory. Sheena had been a mistake, but he couldn't see it at the time. She'd been riding high on the pop charts, and he'd been breaking out in country. They'd partied hard and crashed even harder. Matt had wanted out of that relationship when he started working with Autumn. Of course, Sheena had turned it all around and painted him as an asshole, and Autumn had stepped in to do damage control. Autumn hadn't wanted anything to do with him romantically, but they'd grown close during that time. She'd been mad at him for the damage to his reputation, and he'd believed there was a little bit of jealousy driving her anger, too.

But that was all a few years back now, and the inevitability of him and Autumn ending up together felt like it faded with every month that passed. They'd grown closer; even she wouldn't deny that. Hell. She hadn't even argued with him on the phone earlier when he'd claimed he was her best friend. But nothing had ever happened between them. Not one single stolen kiss, not even a drunken one. He blew out a sigh. He'd never let go of the idea that one day they'd be together. He didn't mind waiting; he believed theirs could be a story like in some old country song—that it'd last a lifetime. He didn't want to wait for something that was never going to happen, though. So far, she'd proved all his predictions wrong. What if he was completely wrong?

He smiled. He wasn't wrong. He couldn't be. The inevitability might feel like it was fading, but why wouldn't it? He hadn't done anything to move things along. Sure, he teased her, but he'd been happy enough to let things move at her pace. If he decided to turn up the heat, her heart would melt sooner—wouldn't it? He was confident in his abilities with the ladies—he'd tested and proved them often enough in the past. That wasn't the same as his ability to win Autumn, though. She was a much greater prize than any he'd ever gone after. He got up and went to stand in front of the windows. Was it time? Time to put himself to the ultimate test? It was. He nodded.

Maybe it was seeing that couple and their kid in the market; maybe it was the fact that his little sister had gotten married last month; maybe it was the fact he and Autumn were about to spend the night here in Seattle, just the two of them with no work to be done. Who knew what it was, but something had shifted. His heart raced. It was time, time to make a start on the rest of his life with the woman he wanted beside him.

Chapter Three

Autumn stared out the window and blew out a sigh as the plane came in to land. She'd had a nice relaxing evening planned for herself—in Nashville—back in her apartment with a bubble bath and a glass of wine or two. Trust Matt to screw it up for her.

"Welcome to Seattle," Zack's voice came through the little speaker beside her head. "It should take us just a few minutes to taxi over to the Signature building, and Matt's already there waiting."

Autumn frowned, wondering how he knew that. She pressed the button on the arm of her seat. "What are you guys doing tonight? Do you want to come out for dinner? My treat." Maybe Zack and Luke would want to join her and Matt. They were good guys, and she hadn't had a chance to check in with them lately. As pilots, they were on the staff, and therefore, technically her responsibility, but they weren't like the other employees, so she tended to let things slip in terms of checking in with them.

There were a few moments' silence and she wondered if they hadn't heard, but then Luke's voice came through. "It's good of you to offer, but you know I'm a sad sack. Angel and I are going to watch a movie together."

Autumn frowned. Luke's fiancée, Angel, was in Summer Lake, California, as far as she knew. Or was she here in Seattle for some reason?

Zack's voice came through next, chuckling. "Can you believe that they both sit and watch the same movie while they're on a video call?"

"Oh!" That would never have occurred to Autumn. She shook her head. "Well, if that's your thing, I wouldn't want to intrude. Say hi to her for me? What about you, Zack?"

"Thanks, but I'm almost as bad as he is. I want to talk to Maria."

Autumn had to laugh. "And here I was thinking that we didn't keep you both away from home too much."

"You don't!" said Luke. "The schedule's fine. We hadn't flown all week till we brought you and Matt out here. It's just that we were supposed to be home tonight."

"Yeah. Sorry about that. It's Matt and his—"

"It's not a problem," said Zack. The plane came to a halt in front of the building, and a moment later, the door from the cockpit opened, and the guys came into the cabin.

Zack smiled at her. "It's not a problem at all. We both love our job, but we love our girls, too, so we do the best we can to be home with them when we said we would—even if we're not actually there."

Autumn smiled. "I hope they know how lucky they are."

Zack laughed. "We know how lucky *we* are. It's not easy to hold down a great job like this and have a woman who understands."

Autumn nodded. "And it's not easy to hang onto a great woman, so I try to make the job as understanding as possible."

"And we appreciate it," said Luke. "It'd be good to take a rain check on the dinner offer—maybe one night when we're in Nashville all week?"

"Sure, we should do that."

Zack opened the door and let the stairs down, then turned back to Autumn with a smile. "We'll look forward to it, but for tonight you enjoy your dinner with Matt. We'll be ready whatever time you want to leave in the morning."

"I'll let you know as soon as I know what time it'll be. West doesn't land till ten tonight. I'm hoping Matt can get hold of him and set something up for as early as possible tomorrow, then we can all get out of here."

"There's no rush on our part," said Luke with a smile.

Autumn let out a short laugh. "Maybe not, but there is on mine. I'm supposed to be on my way home right now. It's typical of Matt to screw things up for all of us."

Zack raised an eyebrow at her. "Didn't he find a replacement drummer?"

Autumn narrowed her eyes at him—for one thing, how did he even know about that, and for another, why was he sticking up for Matt? "He did."

Zack smiled. "So, he's solving a problem, not causing one, right?"

Autumn stared at him.

He shrugged and gave her a half smile. "He's a good guy."

She blew out a sigh. "He might have you charmed, but he's a pain in the ass, is what he is."

Luke smiled at her, too. "So, at least let him buy you dinner to make up for being a pain?"

She scowled at them, wondering why they were talking him up. "He is buying me dinner. I just thought the two of you might want to come along, so I don't have to endure his company all by myself."

Zack laughed. "We wouldn't want to get in the way."

"Of what?"

Zack shrugged and gestured to the steps. "Of the work you two have to do."

She raised an eyebrow at him as she passed him.

"To get a new drummer lined up," added Luke hastily.

A golf cart was waiting at the bottom of the steps. Autumn sat in front next to the driver, expecting to wait while the guys closed up the plane, but when they came down, Zack smiled at her as he placed her bag on the cart. "There's no need to wait. Matt's waiting for you. You guys have a great night."

She wanted to argue, wanted to tell him that there was no rush—Matt could wait. But somehow, she felt as though that would be protesting too much. She'd tried to get them to come out for dinner; they'd said no. It was no big deal. Zack was right. There was no point in her waiting for them just to go their separate ways in the parking lot instead of out here.

She shrugged. "Okay. I'll let you know what time we'll be ready to leave as soon as I figure it out."

"Thanks."

She nodded at the guy driving the golf cart, and he pulled away. She clutched her purse to her chest. This was crazy. She was going to meet Matt, to have dinner with him—as they'd done probably hundreds of times before. So, why was her heart beating extra fast? Maybe it was her suppressed anger and irritation at this whole situation? She should be on her way home. She sucked in a deep breath and let it out slowly. She was hardly going to accept the possibility that it was her suppressed attraction to the damned man, was she? Yes, she could admit it. He drove her freaking nuts! In all the ways she bitched about—but mostly because he did things to her, to her mind and to her treacherous body which reacted in highly unreasonable ways whenever he got close. It was ridiculous; mostly, it was irrelevant—she'd never get involved with him. He was the label's biggest artist, and besides, he was totally unsuitable as boyfriend material. But she couldn't train her dumb body to accept the logic of any of that. She prided herself on being a smart, savvy, take-no-shit businesswoman. But the woman part of her wanted Matt McConnell, just like most every other woman on the planet did.

She closed her eyes briefly as the golf cart came to a stop outside the doors. She'd managed to keep that part of her locked up ever since she and Matt had started working together years ago. He teased her, but that had more to do with his ego than it did with anything he might feel for her. He was so used to women falling at his feet and into his bed, that she merely presented a novelty. A challenge at best. And she had to remind herself of that whenever he turned on the charm. He'd no doubt do it tonight. It'd be just one more test. A duel between her professionalism and his ego. She'd win, as she always did—even if sometimes she lay awake at night wondering what it would be like if she let him win just once.

The doors slid open, and there he was. Damn. She couldn't blame herself for finding him attractive. His cocky grin got her every time, but that was only part of it. His eyes sparkled with mischief—sometimes she wondered if it was lust that shone in them, too. But even if it did, it was only because she was a female with a pulse. His face was so handsome, whether he'd let his beard grow in, like he had now, or he was clean-shaven, he had one of those faces it was hard to drag your eyes away from, and eyes that locked with yours and dared you to discover what might happen if you came closer instead of looking away. He wasn't a big guy, at least not like the muscle-bound Carter. He was muscled, but lean. Right now, his black T-shirt stretched across his chest, hiding the six-pack she knew was beneath. His jeans showed off his muscular thighs, and she knew without needing to see, that they hugged his biteable ass. Even his black boots added to the overall impression of guy-most-likely-to-cause-panties-to-drop.

She got a grip. Her panties would be staying firmly in place, thank you very much. Even if they were a little warmer than they'd been a few moments ago.

He grinned and waved at her, then started out to greet her. The guy who'd driven the cart got her bag, but Matt took it from him with a smile and somehow managed to tip him at the same time. She wanted to be mad at him—it was her place to do that, but the guy was grinning. Matt was such a charmer, and if she opened her mouth, she'd come off as the bitch. Instead, she gave him a grudging smile. "Thanks."

"Thank you! I'm sorry. I know this isn't ideal for you."

She raised an eyebrow as she followed him into the building. "Did I hear that right? Did you just apologize? Does this mean that you are aware that you're not the center of the universe? That I might have had plans of my own and you might have inconvenienced me?"

He stopped walking and looked into her eyes. "Yeah." There was something different about him. He wasn't his usual grinning, cocky and arrogant self.

Immediately, she was worried. "Are you okay?" She touched his arm instinctively.

He looked down at her hand, and to her surprise, he covered it with his own. "I'm okay." He gave her a rueful smile. "I dunno, Autumn Breese. Maybe I'm tired, maybe I'm getting old, but ..."

She held her breath, wondering what he was about to say. Was there something wrong? Was he about to drop the cocky cowboy act and be real with her about something that was going on with him?

No.

He grinned. "But I ain't lost it yet. I know you're pissed at me for making you come here, and I want us to have a fun night, so I'll apologize, say all the things you want to hear, so you'll come out with me." He waggled his eyebrows. "Maybe we'll have a few too many, and I'll finally make it into your bed."

She pursed her lips—if only to cover the way her body reacted to the thought of him finally making it into her bed.

"No?" He raised an eyebrow and gave her his sexy grin. It was the one he used in photo shoots. How bad was it that she knew all his grins and the meaning and purpose behind each of them and when he was most likely to use them?

She shook her head. "You promised me dinner."

His smile was more genuine now. "I did. You're going to love this little Vietnamese place; it's not fancy, but it's real."

She had to smile. "Just like me."

He'd started walking again and looked over his shoulder at her. "You're the most real person I've ever known, but you're fancy."

"I am not," she said with a laugh as they made their way across the parking lot.

He set her bag down next to a Camry, and she had to wonder whether he'd extended the rental by himself. "Yes, you are. You're the consummate professional. You always wear the right things, say the right things, do the right things. You always have everything just so."

"That doesn't make me fancy. I think of fancy as being pretentious."

He turned back to face her and took hold of her shoulders. "Hell, no! That's not what I mean. To me, fancy is perfect. It's beautiful. If something's fancy, then everything's right, without it being an effort. Fancy is upscale, but naturally so. There's nothing forced about fancy."

She had to laugh. "Okay. Good to know." Her smile faded. "And that's how you see me?"

He held her gaze as he nodded. For a moment, she got lost in his big brown eyes, reveling in the knowledge that he thought of her that way. The way he looked back at her, the feel of his hands on her shoulders; it'd be so easy to get lost in that feeling, to give in and … She turned away abruptly and went around to the passenger door. "Can we go to the hotel first? I want to get changed."

He looked at her over the roof of the car, but she opened the door and got inside. This was no time to go falling for his ways. Just because they were alone, away from home, away from work, it didn't mean she should let her guard down. One lapse—one night—with Matt could never be just that. They had to work together.

As she slid into the passenger seat, she saw an iced caramel macchiato sitting in the cup holder and smiled to herself.

Chapter Four

Matt checked his watch. It was almost seven forty-five. One of the many things he appreciated about Autumn was that she didn't like to waste time. When they'd gotten back here to the apartment, she'd told him to give her half an hour, and she'd be ready to go for dinner. He'd wanted to show her into her room—so he could see her reaction to the flowers and goodies he'd gotten her, but she'd taken her bag from him at the door and told him she'd text when she was ready. He hoped that she'd realize the coffee and doughnuts and especially the tulips were from him.

He jumped to his feet at the sound of a knock on his door. He bit the inside of his cheek in an attempt to stop a huge grin from spreading across his face at the sight of her. She was gorgeous. He knew all her looks—from the crisp business suits to the fancy gowns she wore to award shows. She looked fantastic in all of them. But standing there in the doorway, he'd swear she looked more beautiful than he'd ever seen her. She was wearing faded blue jeans and a deep blue long-sleeved T-shirt. It was such a simple look, yet she took his breath away.

She raised an eyebrow at him. "Can I come in? Or are you ready to go?"

He pulled himself together. "Come on in a minute. I just need to grab my wallet."

She came into the apartment and walked straight over to the wall of windows. "I like this place. The view is great."

"I'm glad you approve."

She turned back to look at him, and his heart raced when she gave him one of her rare, gentle smiles. "I approve of the coffee and doughnuts, too. Thank you."

He shrugged, trying to look bashful, but not sure he pulled it off. "It's the least I could do. I know you don't want to be here."

He couldn't fathom the look in her eyes when she said, "It's not that I don't want to, it's just ..." She shook her head. "It's not what I planned. It doesn't ..." She shook her head again. "It's fine. You did well setting it up. We need to get you a drummer, and we all know West is the best."

He chuckled; it was easier to go with her play on words about Weston than it would be to try and figure out what she'd meant when she said that it wasn't that she didn't want to be here. "He is, and from what he's said, I think it'll be a straightforward meeting. He wants back in. We just need to iron out the details."

Autumn nodded. "Good. Then hopefully we can get done before lunchtime and get back. We'll need to get him to Nashville as soon as we can as well."

"If I know West, he might come with us."

"That'd be ideal. Then we can work him up a contract, get him signed, and get back to work."

"Yep." Matt was eager to work out the details. He was looking forward to working with West and to seeing how he gelled with the other guys, but that wasn't his top priority for tonight. Tonight, he wanted to forget about work, forget that he and Autumn worked together. He wanted to enjoy an evening with her as just a guy and a girl going out for dinner. If he had his way, it'd be more than just dinner, but he wasn't holding out much hope on that front. She'd knocked him back for years. He'd never give up, but he knew better than to set himself up for disappointment, too. "Anyway," he picked up his wallet. "No more talk about work for tonight. When a guy buys you flowers and takes you out to dinner, you might take the hint that he's got more than work on his mind."

He went to the door and held it open for her.

She pursed her lips as she passed him. "I thought we were going out as friends? Are you really such an asshole that you'd hit on your friend?"

He followed her to the elevator and deliberately leaned in close as he reached past her to hit the button. He breathed in the scent of her and closed his eyes briefly, trying to push down the lust that bubbled up inside him. "One day, you'll figure out how hard I've worked not to be an asshole around you, Autumn Breese. If I were an asshole, I would have hit on you relentlessly from the day I met you. We would never have become friends."

For once, she didn't have a comeback. She just looked up at him, searching his eyes. He looked back into hers, wishing he could tell her without words how he really felt.

They both jumped when the elevator arrived with a ding.

As they rode down to the lobby, he reached out and touched her arm. "Sorry, baby girl. You know, your friendship is about the most important thing in the world to me. I wouldn't do anything to put it at risk."

She nodded slowly but didn't say anything.

Matt was relieved when they stepped out into the fresh air. He was afraid he may have just lied to her. If the two of them were to ever cross the line, that would put their friendship at risk, and he knew it. But he wasn't sure he'd be able to resist if the opportunity arose.

He turned right out of the building and made his way down Second Street. For once, he didn't know what to say to her.

She was a few inches shorter than him, but she matched his stride easily. They walked in silence for a little while until she looked up at him. He didn't know if it was the outfit, the jeans and T-shirt look, or the fact that her long dark hair fell loose around her shoulders, but she looked younger, fresher somehow than she usually did. Even more so when she smiled. "That was a sweet thing to do. Thank you."

"What?"

"The flowers."

He smiled. "I wasn't sure you noticed. I knew you wouldn't miss the coffee and donuts."

She smiled back. "They had to be you—you know my addiction and my favorite brands. But the tulips ...?"

He shrugged. "I know about those, too."

She frowned. "How?"

"I pay attention."

"Why?"

He slung his arm around her shoulders as they walked. "Would you believe me if I said because I care?"

He felt her tense and wondered what she was going to say. She surprised him when she reached up and squeezed his hand. "You're not all bad, are you?"

He laughed. "I'm not bad at all. You should give me a chance—you might be surprised how good I am."

He shouldn't have been surprised that she took that the wrong way. She made a face and wriggled out from under his arm. "How many times do I have to tell you? Hitting on your friends is an asshole move. I don't need to try you for myself. I've heard enough glowing reports from enough wide-eyed women over the years about just how *good* you are."

He blew out a sigh. "I didn't mean it that way. Why are you always so ready to think of me as just some guy who wants into your pants?"

She shook her head. "Because I know you too well."

He wasn't going to get anywhere going down this path with her. He couldn't make her see him as a good guy who cared about her. He grinned. "Maybe the problem is, you don't know me well enough?" He waggled his eyebrows. "But we could change that—anytime you like."

She stopped walking and held his gaze for a long moment. He thought he'd gone too far. Was she about to tell him where he could shove it?

No.

Instead, she surprised the hell out of him. "Maybe one day we should."

"What?!"

She looked less sure of herself than she usually did. "You heard me. Maybe one day I should put you to the test. Find out just how good you really are, and then we can put all this behind us."

"You're not serious?" His heart was pounding in his chest—hoping against hope that she was serious.

She laughed. "Of course, I'm not. I just wanted to call your bluff. You wouldn't know what to do with me if I said yes, would you?"

Matt swallowed, hard. He could hardly tell her that he knew exactly what he'd like to do with her—that he'd spent far too many nights lying awake thinking about her and what they could do. He gave her his cocky grin. "Maybe it's time for me to call your bluff? Do you really believe that I wouldn't?"

Her eyes widened, and she started walking again. "Where is this restaurant, anyway? I thought you said it was just around the corner from the apartment."

He smirked to himself as he set off after her and pointed. "It is. It's just there, look."

Once they were seated at a table by the window and the server had taken their order, he smiled at her. "Should we call a truce?"

She smiled and nodded. "Yeah. We probably should. Sorry about that. It's just that sometimes I get so mad at you. I feel like we could be real friends if you'd just drop all the other stuff. Especially since you don't mean it. It's just a habit for you to try to talk women into bed."

He put his hand over his heart and gave her a hurt look. "Come on, Autumn. That's not fair. I've been a good boy for a long time." He didn't want to point out that he'd been a very good boy for a very long time. Sure, he took advantage of the perks of being a country singer, but the eager women who always surrounded him and the band had lost their appeal over time. More often than not, he turned them away. He'd dance with them, have drinks with them, but when it came down to taking them to his room, he backed out, bid them goodnight, and went to bed alone—usually to lie there thinking about Autumn.

She made a face. "Pft. I guess that's your play on the word good again. I'm sure you are."

"I didn't mean it that way. I mean, I'm not like I used to be."

"Whatever. Shall we just leave it at the fact that we're calling a truce? Admit that you're not interested in me in that way, so you don't need to keep up the flirty act?"

He sucked in a deep breath. The sensible thing to do would be to agree with her. Let it go and try to have fun with the evening. Trouble was, he couldn't let it go. He couldn't let her go on believing that he wasn't interested in her. She really thought that all his jokes and quips and lines were just that—that they were born of habit and not of real attraction?

"I'll go with the truce, but I have to set you straight about the other part." He folded his arms on the table and leaned forward to look deep into her eyes. "I've always had you down as one smart lady, but if you honestly believe that I'm not interested in you in that way, then you're dumber than a box of rocks, baby girl."

Her smile faded as she looked back into his eyes. "Are you serious?" Her voice was barely more than a whisper.

He nodded and reached across the table to take hold of her hand. "Dead serious. I've never been more serious about anything in my life. You ... you're everything. You're gorgeous, you're smart, you rule my world." He smiled. "In a very real sense as well as the way you blow me away."

She squeezed his hand briefly. "I thought ... You just play the game ... You do it with everyone ... You ..."

He lowered his head and looked up at her from under his lashes. "You can't tell the difference? Sure, I'm the world's biggest flirt, but you and me? That's different. There's a power play; I'm not denying that. But the biggest factor is that I'm nuts about you. I tell you that almost every day."

She looked so vulnerable leaning toward him; all her edge was gone, she looked confused. He wanted to believe that she looked eager to believe him, but he didn't know what was going on behind her big blue eyes. "It's not just a game?" she asked eventually.

"Hell no. I mean, sure, we play it as a game but ..." He shrugged. "I'm laying it all out there for you, baby girl."

He wondered if she'd throw it back at him, turn this into a joke and move on in the safest way possible. It might be best if she did, but he was tired of the game. He wanted to make it real. He held his breath as he waited for her next words.

"It could never work. We work together."

He frowned. "And we work well together. You can't deny that. If we made as good a team as a couple as we do as a working partnership, we'd be amazing."

She held his gaze for a long moment. "But what about when it ended?"

His heart was racing in his chest, and he could hear the blood rushing in his temples. Was she really considering it? If she was, she needed to know how he saw it—how he hoped it could work out. "What if it didn't?"

Her eyebrows knit together in confusion.

He'd come this far; he might as well spell it out. "What if we got together, and it never ended?"

She let go of his hand and sat back as if she'd been slapped. And of course, at that moment, the server appeared with their food.

Chapter Five

Matt had been right. The food was fabulous. Autumn loved Vietnamese food. She'd barely been able to appreciate it though. Her mind was whirling, and her stomach was doing back-flips the whole time they sat there. If he was playing his usual games, then he'd won this one, hands down. He'd thrown her for a loop. He must be playing. He couldn't be serious—could he?

She sipped the rest of her Cosmo while she waited for him to return from the bathroom. She shouldn't have had that last one, but they were going down so easily, and if ever a girl needed a drink, it was on the night that the guy she'd had a huge crush on for years told her that they could make a great couple if she were willing to give it a try—and that her fears about how them breaking up would affect their working relationship would be unfounded if they didn't ever break up. What did that even mean? Two people who got together and never broke up? They'd be together forever. "Pft!" She couldn't help the little snort of disbelief that escaped her lips.

The waiter turned at the sound and smiled at her. A few moments later, he reappeared with yet another Cosmo. She held up her hand and shook her head. She'd had one too many already, but the guy smiled so eagerly. The staff here had been wonderful.

"On the house," he said with a smile.

It'd be churlish to turn him down. Instead, she took it with a smile and a thank you and drained the last one.

She needed to get it together. Needed to get her guard back up. Whatever Matt was playing at, it couldn't be as simple as he was saying—that he was attracted to her and wanted them to give it a shot. Could it? Everyone had told her for years that he liked her. Her sister always teased her that it was inevitable— that she knew Autumn liked him, too. She made a face to herself and took a slug of her fresh drink. So what? Of course, she was attracted to him—she didn't know many women who weren't. She sat back in her seat and looked out the window at the people scurrying by on the busy street. She couldn't get involved with him. Even if he were for real that he wanted to. That crap about not breaking up was just that—crap! Everyone broke up, especially in Nashville. It would just be too difficult afterward. How would they work together afterward? How would she feel when she saw him going back to his usual ways after he'd been with her? Could she trust herself to still treat him as nothing more than one of the artists? She pursed her lips. Of course, she couldn't. She was close to all of them. No.

Even if he was for real, there was too much on the line. She couldn't risk their working relationship for the sake of the label. And she wouldn't risk their friendship for her own sake. Yeah, he was a pain in the ass, but he was her pain in the ass, and she couldn't imagine losing the bond they shared.

She glanced over at the men's room, wondering what was taking him so long and had to smile when she saw him standing at the servers' station talking to two of the waiters. That was just who he was. He had a kind word for everyone. More than that, he had a way of making people feel special.

She doubted the waiters knew who he was—or would care if they did. They weren't awed in the presence of a country music superstar. They were just enjoying the company of an appreciative customer. A gregarious customer who was taking a minute to make them smile.

He really was a good guy. For all his jokes and innuendo about being good in bed, she knew from experience that he was a decent, genuine human being. A little shiver ran down her spine. She'd love to experience just how good he was in bed, too. If you took away all their history, all the complications that made it impossible, she was still a woman. A young woman who had wants and needs. And if she was honest, those needs hadn't been met in a long time. She was too busy with work to date. And even if she could find the time, she wouldn't date anyway. She pressed her lips together, and a heavy ball of realization settled in her stomach. She wouldn't want to date anyone else—because she was too hung up on Matt! Had she really not known that? Or had she successfully ignored it until right this minute?

She frowned. Was it just the Cosmos talking? There'd been quite a few of them.

"Excuse me?"

She turned to look at a guy who had approached the table. She wanted to laugh. It was as if the universe heard her musing that she wouldn't want to date anyone else and had sent her a *very* hot guy to test her theory. Damn! She'd love to use him in a music video. He had short dark hair, big, blue eyes, and a chiseled jawline. He had the look of a marine and the body to match. She pulled herself together. "Yes?"

"I'm sorry to just barge in on you like this, but are you … you're Autumn Breese, aren't you?"

She sat back in her seat and looked up at him. She was used to the people she was with being recognized. It went with the territory when all your friends were famous singers, but it was rare that anyone approached her. She nodded. "I am."

The guy grinned and slid into Matt's seat across from her. "You're amazing!"

She stared at him for a moment. "Thank you." Was all she could think to say.

"Sorry." The guy held out his hand, and she shook with him. "I'm Kent Eddy. I'm a huge fan. I followed your sister's career, and since she retired, I've followed you. You've done such great things with McAdam Records."

She smiled. "I'm just the one who holds it all together; it's the artists who do great things."

The guy shook his head. "They wouldn't be anything without you. There are hundreds, thousands of talented singers out there. You're the one who finds the best and guides and drives their careers."

She smiled. "Thanks. It's nice to be appreciated."

"I'm sure. Most people only see the stars. I'm more interested in the brains," he stopped and let his gaze run over her, "and the beauty who launches them."

"Is this guy bothering you?"

They both looked up when Matt came to stand over the table.

"I hope not." Kent caught Autumn's eye. "Sorry. I didn't mean to intrude on your business dinner." He smiled at Matt. "But you can't blame a guy for wanting to talk to your boss here."

Matt scowled at him. "I can't blame you, but I can ask you to back off. Tonight, she's not my boss."

"Oh! Shit! I'm sorry, man." Kent got to his feet. "I didn't know. I had no clue."

Autumn scowled at Matt, but he slid back into his seat and looked up at Kent. "That's okay. You weren't to know."

Kent gave Autumn an apologetic smile. "It was great to meet you."

"You, too." Autumn gave him her best smile. She was mad at Matt for shooing him off like that.

Kent looked at Matt. "You're a lucky guy."

Matt grinned at him. "I sure am."

Once he'd gone, Autumn scowled at Matt. "What the hell are you playing at?"

Matt's grin faded. "I thought I was rescuing you."

She blew out a sigh. "Rescuing me from the hot guy who thinks I'm amazing?"

It was Matt's turn to scowl. "Err, yeah. Why not, since you're out for dinner with me?"

She wanted to stay mad at him, but she couldn't help the warm feeling that spread through her at the thought that maybe he was a teeny bit jealous. She smiled. "So, you do care?"

"How many times and how many ways do I have to say it?"

She shrugged, vaguely aware that that last Cosmo was a really bad idea. "Maybe a couple more?" she said with a smile.

He smiled back and reached across the table to take hold of her hand. "I'll tell you as many times as you like if you think there's a chance you might end up believing me."

"There may be a teeny chance." She squeezed his hand. The sensible little voice in the back of her mind was screaming—asking her what the hell she thought she was playing at, but she didn't want to listen to it, didn't want to answer. What she wanted was to enjoy this feeling just for a while. Feeling that Matt wanted her was intoxicating—and when you added that to the job the Cosmos were already doing, she didn't want to stop.

"Do you want to get out of here?"

She met his gaze and knew her decision was made. When his eyes locked with hers, she was lost. Those eyes had always invited her to come closer, and for the first time, her better judgment wasn't strong enough to come to her rescue. Her senses were too busy enjoying the Cosmos to ask her to come back to them, and in that perfect storm moment, she nodded. "Yeah. I do."

Matt got to his feet, and she had to laugh. "I know you're in a hurry, but don't you think we should pay first?"

He chuckled. "I already took care of it. I was settling the bill when I noticed that guy harassing you."

"He wasn't harassing me. He was very complimentary, actually. He recognized me for the genius that I am. He knows that all of you would be nothing without me."

Matt made a face at her. "And you think we don't know that?"

"Oh." She'd been expecting that to ruffle his ego, but he shook his head.

"We know that we owe it all to you. And we try to tell you often enough." He shot a glance at Kent, who raised a hand as he watched them leave. "It's a shame that you'll take it as a compliment from a complete stranger but won't even listen when I tell you."

She looked up at him, wondering whether he was serious, and he smiled and wrapped his arm around her shoulders. "We need to work on that."

"On what?"

"On you being more receptive to me."

She chuckled. "I'm feeling very receptive right now." She was, too. She'd probably regret this for a long time to come, but right now all she wanted to do was to get Matt back to the apartment and find out just how good he was—and prove just how receptive she was feeling. She slid her arm around his waist.

He winked at her and landed a peck on her lips and asked, "Then why are we still here?"

Chapter Six

Matt fumbled with his key card when they got back to the apartment building. He couldn't believe this was really happening. Autumn leaned against the wall and smiled at him. "Do you need a hand?"

"No, thanks." He pushed the door open and gestured for her to go in ahead of him.

She went straight to the elevators and pushed the button. "Have you ever done it in an elevator?"

He met her gaze and shook his head. "No." He smiled. "Or should my answer be not yet?"

She laughed. "We won't be changing your answer tonight. We'd have to be in a private building before we could risk that. I'm already worried enough about that Kent guy."

Matt frowned. It was obvious that she'd had one too many, but he'd thought she was just a little tipsy. Now it seemed that she wasn't even making sense. "What do you mean?"

"I'm pretty sure he snapped a photo of us before we left. Right when you landed a kiss on me."

Matt shrugged. "Does it matter?"

"Not for me. I don't have millions of adoring fans needing me to remain single, so they can fantasize about how someday I'll be theirs."

"My fans don't need that. They'll be thrilled to know we're together."

Autumn made a face and then the elevator arrived, and they stepped inside. When the doors closed, he turned to her and put his hands on her shoulders, backing her against the wall. "Do you know how long I've waited for this?"

She shrugged. "Just as long as I have."

"You haven't waited for this; you've never considered giving me a chance till now."

"You honestly believe that? You think I'm the ice queen who's immune to your charms? Well, uh-uh, Mister. Think again. It's only my exterior that's icy. Underneath, I'm warm." She smiled. "And further down, I'm hot." She ran her tongue over her bottom lip, and that was all he could take.

He traced the trail her tongue had left with his own. "I know you're hot. You're so damned hot."

She shook her head. "I meant I'm hot for you, right now."

He sank his fingers into her hair and covered her mouth with his own. The blood was surging in his veins, making him ache for her. His cock strained against his zipper as he leaned his weight against her and began to explore her with his tongue. Her arms came up around his shoulders, and she rocked her hips against him. The feel of her lithe body drove him wild, and he kissed her more deeply still, desperate for the moment when he could thrust more than his tongue inside her.

The elevator came to a halt, and they broke apart breathlessly. He took hold of her hand and led her toward his apartment. She stopped as they passed her room, and she tugged on his hand. "In here."

He nodded and waited while she unlocked the door. Once they were inside, she backed him up against it and nibbled her way up his neck. He forced his hands to remain still at his sides and let the shivers roll through him. When she reached his lips, she looked up into his eyes.

"Do you want me, Matt?"

He closed his arms around her waist. "Hell, yeah, I want you. I've wanted you since the first time you blew into that tour meeting. You kicked asses and took names and knocked that whole thing into shape in no time. I got a hard-on watching you take charge and," he rocked his hips against her, "I've had it all this time."

She raised an eyebrow at him. "You don't need to make stuff up and bullshit me. This is happening. I just want you to be honest with me."

He bit her bottom lip and ran his hands up her sides, resisting the temptation to cup her breasts. He knew once he did that there'd be no more talking for a while, and he still had a few things to say. "You want me to be honest?"

She nodded.

"Okay. I was sitting in Anton's office wondering if my first big tour was going to shit because he was useless and kept dropping the ball. I got a call from Ashley Devlin to tell me that Autumn Breese was on her way over and was going to pull the tour together. I told the guys that we had a hard-ass bitch from the label coming in to shake things up and that we needed to make nice with you no matter how bad you were because you'd get things done. Half an hour later, you blew into that office, and you blew me away. You were wearing a navy-blue suit with a white blouse. There was a split in your skirt that I couldn't take my eyes off of—wishing that it went just a little bit higher so I could see more of the best set of legs I ever laid eyes on—legs that I later told Levi that I wanted to feel wrapped around me. You put Anton in his place. You sorted out the next three dates before we left that office, and I had a boner for you the whole time."

"The next time I saw you, I asked you to go to dinner. You totally ignored the bit about it being me and you—a date—and agreed to go to dinner and spent the whole time talking about the tour. I tried and I tried, and you blew me off at every turn."

She rolled her eyes. "You were seeing Sheena."

"I broke up with Sheena because I couldn't think about anything but you."

Autumn took a step back, but he tightened his arms around her and drew her back to him. "It's true. I've wanted you for all this time. I've tried, and I've waited patiently. And I've tried some more. I've never given up."

She cocked her head to one side. "You're serious, aren't you?"

He nodded. "Deadly serious."

"Wow."

She turned away from him and went to sit on the sofa.

This wasn't going the way he'd hoped. He hadn't wanted to rush it, but he hadn't planned on sitting and talking either, but she needed to understand. He needed her to know that this meant something to him. That he'd waited a long time for it. He frowned. If she thought that he just wanted to screw her and be done—then why was she up for it? What did it mean to her?

He went and sat down facing her. "When I said all that, I thought it'd help you understand how I feel. I didn't mean it to be a mood killer."

She gave him a faint smile. "Sorry. It's a lot to process."

He nodded, feeling the moment slipping away. He reached out and ran his hand up her calf. "We could process it in the morning?"

She smiled. "Yeah."

"Did I blow it?"

She nodded slowly. "Yeah. Well, no. You didn't blow it. I think I did. A long time ago."

"Nah. You just made me wait. That's probably a good thing. Gave me a chance to do some growing up in the meantime."

She ran her gaze over him. "And you grew into a fine man."

His heart felt as though it might beat out of his chest when she met his gaze and spoke again.

"I'll probably regret telling you this, but I'm not immune to your charms. I can't lie and say I don't want you ..."

He edged closer, sensing that this was the invitation he'd waited for so long. He planted his hands on either side of her hips and lowered his head. There was heat in her eyes as she lifted her lips to his. When they met, a rush of heat seared his veins. Her fingers tangled in his hair, and he kissed her deeply, tasting her, exploring her, loving the way her tongue met his as she kissed him back. They sank down on the sofa, limbs tangling, bodies writhing. Little moans escaped from her as he ground his cock between her legs, wishing for the first time tonight that she'd worn a skirt instead of jeans.

He let his hands roam over her and moaned himself when she cupped his ass and rocked him against her. Her legs came up and wrapped themselves around his back. Just like he'd wanted them to since that day in Anton's office years ago.

She pulled her head back and looked up into his eyes. Her blue eyes were glazed with lust; his cock ached to be inside her. He'd waited so long for this moment, he couldn't wait much longer. But she shook her head and put a hand to his shoulder, pushing him back.

"We can't do this."

Damn! He wanted to push her back down, reclaim her mouth, persuade her with his body that they could and they should. Instead, he sat back and drew in a deep breath.

"Why not, baby girl?"

"I'm drunk."

He pursed his lips. It was true, and he knew it. Was he really going to take advantage of her?

"You're sober enough to know that you're drunk."

She glared at him, and for a moment, he feared he was about to receive a tongue lashing of the kind he didn't want. Her expression softened. "Yeah. I guess I am. But if you've waited this long, what's the harm in waiting a little longer?"

He shrugged. She had a point. "I like to live in the moment?" He ventured.

She gave him a rueful smile. "So do I, but we always have to keep an eye on the future. Everything we do today affects tomorrow." She touched his shoulder. "I'm not saying I don't want to. Just that I don't want to right now. I need to think this through—and so do you."

He shook his head rapidly. "I've done all the thinking about this I need to. I've had years to think about it." He blew out a sigh. "But I can wait. How long?"

She laughed. "I don't know. A while."

He nodded sadly. "However long you need."

She held his gaze for a moment. "It's for the best. We both need to be sure."

"I am sure."

She shrugged. "Maybe."

They both jumped when his cell phone rang. Matt closed his eyes, cursing the timing.

Autumn got up from the sofa. "You should get that. It might be West."

Chapter Seven

When they arrived at the airport the next morning, Autumn excused herself and went to the ladies' room while they waited for the plane to be ready. She ran her wrists under the water and looked herself in the eye in the mirror. "What are you playing at?" she asked herself and shrugged in reply.

Part of her wished she'd kept her mouth shut last night. She'd wanted Matt more than she'd ever wanted a guy. It would've been so easy to give in to what they'd both wanted. But she was a pragmatist. There would be consequences, and she needed to think them through before she could go there.

West's phone call had changed the course of the night. Matt had suggested that they meet with him at eight o'clock this morning and had told him they were heading back to Nashville as soon as they were done. As he'd predicted, West had suggested that he should come along with them—and so they could hold their meeting on the plane. It worked out for the best, though it made Autumn uncomfortable. She'd rather have had those few hours alone with Matt. She'd wanted to talk to him, to figure out where they stood. Just because they weren't going to jump each other's bones straight away, that didn't mean they couldn't start something—start interacting in a different way.

Now, she felt as though she had something to hide from the others. She didn't want West to get the impression that there was anything going on between them. She didn't want Luke and Zack to know. She blew out a sigh and turned off the faucet. There wasn't anything going on between them. Not yet. She didn't know how to handle this. She didn't want to let her professionalism slip. She needed to know how she felt and where she and Matt stood before she knew how to present it to anyone else. She dried her hands and pushed a strand of hair off her cheek. Maybe it was going to be too difficult? Maybe she should write the whole thing off as a mistake. A close call.

She let herself back out and looked around the waiting area. She could see Luke and Zack through the windows, walking back across the tarmac. There was no sign of West and ... oh ... there was Matt. He was leaning against the wall opposite the ladies' room. He had his hands in his pockets, and he wore his earnest smile; the one he used in interviews when he'd been nominated for an award. It went with his, *I'm just a good ole hard working boy trying to do the best I can, and it's an honor to be recognized* speech.

He held her gaze as he pushed away from the wall and came toward her. "I wish we'd had more time to talk," he said when he reached her. "I'll wait as long as you need me to, but how do you want to play it?"

She shrugged. "I don't know. I don't know what to think. I don't know what to say."

He winked at her. "I'm with you. I don't know how to act in front of West and the guys."

She pursed her lips. "Just act the way you always do."

"You're disowning me? You don't want anyone to know?"

Autumn's heart raced. *He* did? She'd been half expecting him to pretend the whole thing had never happened. "There's nothing to know."

He frowned. "Yeah, there is. We're starting something here. Aren't we?"

"I don't know."

West came out hurrying toward them. "Looks like we're ready to go. There are two pilots standing by your gear."

Autumn forced a bright smile. "Good. Let's get out of here."

She followed West to where Luke and Zack were waiting. Matt walked a few steps behind her. She felt his hand brush the back of her arm and turned to look at him. His eyes were serious, for once.

"I get you need some time to wrap your head around it, but you can't hide me forever," he said in a low voice.

She nodded. They were almost to the others, and she didn't want to talk about it in front of them—she didn't know what to say anyway.

West was in great form. He was excited to get back to Nashville and get back to work. While the plane taxied out to the runway, and even while they took off, he regaled them with stories of his time in Panama. It sounded like he'd had a blast. He'd traveled throughout Central and South America but had made his home base in Boquete, a town in the highlands near the border with Costa Rica.

Matt got along great with the guy and was thrilled at the prospect of working with him, but right now, he wished he wasn't here. He'd rather West had said that he'd follow them to Nashville later in the week—so that he and Autumn could have had this plane ride home to themselves. He needed to talk to her, needed to persuade her that he respected her decision not to go there last night, but that it didn't mean they weren't going to go there at all.

Instead of talking to him about where things could go between the two of them, she seemed intent on talking to West about his travels. Apparently, the town where he'd lived was famous for its coffee, so, of course, she wanted to hear all about it. While Matt had thought she'd want to get straight down to business and talk about bringing West back into the band, she was more interested in his offer to get a friend to send a shipment of coffee.

He stared out the window and watched the ferry leaving the port, heading for Bainbridge Island, he'd guess. He wanted to interrupt them and get down to talking business, but he knew better than that. Autumn would handle this however she saw fit—and wouldn't thank him for trying to steer her in any other direction.

Eventually she and West exhausted the topic of Panama and its coffee, and West grinned at Matt.

"So, what are you working on? Where do I fit into all of this? And …" he grinned at Autumn. "Before she gets me to sign my life away, do you think Corbin would be interested in taking me on?"

Matt had to smile at that. Corbin was his manager, a veteran of the country music industry and an old friend of Clay McAdam's. He was the best in the business, as far as Matt was concerned. So much so that he often referred to Corbin as his fairy godfather. "We can talk to him."

Autumn met his gaze for the first time since they'd taken off. "That'd be great, thanks. It'll make life easier for all of us if Corbin's involved."

Matt nodded. Corbin was a great guy. He managed the rest of the band and had a great working relationship with Autumn and the other label execs, too. The press had quizzed Matt several times early on in his career as to whether Corbin could truly represent his interests since he was such a good friend of the label's owner. Matt had never doubted him for a second. He'd never admitted publicly that Corbin had been Clay's suggestion—he knew how that would sound. But he also knew that Clay had had his best interests at heart. He'd been young and green and totally naïve.

When Clay wanted to sign him to McAdam Records, he'd been so thrilled that he'd have signed whatever Clay and the label execs wanted him to. He'd believed he didn't need a manager. But Clay had insisted—to the point where he'd told him he wouldn't sign him at all without a manager. When Matt hadn't known where to start, Clay had given him a list of possible candidates, people in the industry he knew and trusted to be fair—people who wouldn't take advantage. Matt had met with four of them—two high powered women, one dry younger guy who had a great reputation for getting his artists the best deal possible, and Corbin. It had been a no-brainer decision to sign with Corbin. He was one of the good old guys. He'd played lead guitar with Clay for years before he retired to spend more time with his family. He'd only returned to Nashville after a nasty divorce, just a year before Matt signed with him.

"Can we set up a meeting with him when we land?" asked West.

"Sure." He smiled at Autumn but spoke to West. "You'll want to get him in your corner before she gets to you. You won't know what hit you otherwise."

He intended it as a joke and kind of a compliment. Autumn was known as a tough negotiator. West chuckled, but Autumn just held his gaze for a moment and then pursed her lips and looked away. Shit! He didn't know what she thought he meant—but she evidently didn't take it as a compliment.

West either didn't notice the tension or stepped in to smooth it over. "All I know is that Corbin's the best, and like Autumn said, it'll make things easier for all of us if he's involved. I know he manages the other guys, too. I'm looking forward to working with them. What do they think of me coming on board?"

Matt blew out a sigh. "I haven't even told them yet. I only heard from Reggie this weekend that he wasn't coming back. I assume he told them before he left." He nodded to himself. He'd have to meet with Levi and Lance as soon as he could—this afternoon if they were free. They both knew West, but he wanted to make sure that they were happy with bringing him on before any deals were signed. He didn't foresee any issues, but he needed to be sure.

"And going back to the question of what he's working on …" There was an edge to Autumn's voice. Matt gave her a puzzled look, but she deliberately avoided his gaze. "He's back in the studio this week finishing the album." When she did turn to him, there was no warmth in her eyes. "How many tracks do you still have to lay down?"

"Five. And I think the single is one of them."

She scowled at him. "We agreed that No Angel is going to be the single."

He shook his head. "You thought that it should be, but like I told you, we're not done yet, and I think you'll agree with me when you hear." He held her gaze, willing her to rise to the bait. They had hours of discussions and debates over matters like this. Some people might call them arguments, but Matt enjoyed them. She'd never overruled him yet, and he doubted that she would, but she made a strong case for her choices that differed from his. It was probably fifty-fifty that he ended up going her way—and it worked out well when he did.

This time she didn't argue. She simply shook her head with an irritated look. "So, hurry up and get them ready for me to hear."

He nodded, disappointed and a little perturbed by her reaction. It looked like his afternoon was going to get real busy. He'd have to talk to Corbin and get him set up to meet with West. He'd have to meet up with Levi and Lance and make sure they were on board with West, but most importantly, he'd have to somehow get Autumn alone for more than a few minutes and figure out what was going on with her—and hopefully, what could go on between the two of them.

Autumn blew out a big sigh when she made it to her office. She sank down into her chair and booted up her computer. She felt unsettled, to say the least. The plane ride home had been uncomfortable. She'd mostly managed to ignore the weird vibes Matt was giving off, but at times, she'd wondered if he was having a dig at her. She'd have to talk to him at some point soon. There was no question about that. But now that they were back in Nashville, she had a whole bunch of other, more pressing, issues to deal with.

She opened her email and scanned her inbox. Lots of issues. She prided herself on her efficiency—which depended in large part in her ability to prioritize. There was a part of her that considered the matter of Matt and her to be top priority, but that part had to take a back seat to business.

Before she allowed herself to open any of her emails, she started to make a list of everything she needed to get done and to prioritize them. That way, when she saw what other people needed from her, she could decide where it fit on her to-do list.

Ten minutes later, she looked up at the sound of a knock on her door. The last thing she needed was an interruption. Her door was always open—at least metaphorically speaking—to the artists and the label staff. It was one of the reasons that McAdam Records did so well; she fostered a collaborative working environment, but some days—like today—it was harder than others to be open to accommodating others' priorities.

"Come in," she called, sounding sharper than she'd intended.

The door swung open, and Clay stood there smiling at her. "How's it going?"

She pursed her lips. "What the hell are you doing here? How did you even get here?"

He gave her his easy smile and came inside, closing the door behind him. "It's nice to see you, too."

She got up with an apologetic smile and came around her desk to greet him with a hug. "Sorry. You caught me off guard. It's great to see you. I just wasn't expecting you. Plus, I had the plane this weekend. So, how did you get here?"

He shrugged and stood back to look her over. "Corbin called and invited us over for the weekend. You already had plans in Montana, so Marianne's son-in-law, Smoke, let us use his jet."

Autumn made a face. "You should have said. I only used the plane because you didn't have any plans to. You take priority. I could have postponed my trip."

Clay shrugged and settled his large frame in the chair across the desk from hers. "It's not a problem. We all got where we needed to go. How was your weekend? How are Summer and Carter and the baby?"

"It was good; they're doing great. Little Penny's adorable."

Clay smiled at that. "Isn't she? I need to get up there again soon. It's been too long."

"I know they'd love to see you." She paused, wondering whether he'd already heard about Reggie leaving.

"Yeah. I'm glad you made it up there." He raised an eyebrow. "I hear you spent the night in Seattle, too?"

Her heart raced. Surely Matt wouldn't have told him about their night—about what had almost happened between them? She nodded cautiously. Hoping Clay would give her more of a clue about what he'd heard before she had to say anything.

He grinned. "I swear Matt is charmed or something. I was concerned, if not totally surprised when I heard about Reggie. But then Matt tells me he's already lined up a replacement, and it's none other than Weston Dailey."

Autumn nodded. "Yeah, it worked out well. I believe he's taking him over to see Corbin this afternoon."

"That's right. He called while we were having brunch."

Autumn nodded again and didn't look away from his curious gaze.

"So, what happens from here?" he asked.

Her heart thudded to a halt. Did he know what happened? Was he asking what she planned to do about Matt—*with* Matt? She raised an eyebrow, hoping he'd elaborate further.

"I'm guessing Matt can get back to finishing the album, no interruptions necessary and then he'll be back out on tour?"

"Yes." She breathed a sigh of relief. "There's no need for any changes or delays. As long as West gets signed with Corbin and we can negotiate a contract quickly, it'll be a seamless transition."

"Good. Anything else I need to know about?"

Her heart raced again, but it was only because she was feeling guilty. If he knew about her and Matt, he wouldn't toy with her like this. He'd ask, she was sure. She shook her head slowly. "No new developments—at least, not that I'm aware of yet. I've only been here a few minutes myself. I need to get caught up. I'd planned to be back in here early this morning. But Matt screwed that up for me, as usual."

Clay chuckled. "I don't know why you're so hard on him. He did you a favor bringing West in. It could have been a major headache and a major delay if we'd had to find a new drummer from scratch. You should take it easy on him—give him a chance, maybe even show him a little appreciation."

She held his gaze for a moment. Did he know? Was he telling her to give Matt a chance on a more personal level? He often joked with her about the two of them getting together, but … She shook her head to clear it of the most inappropriate images that started to crowd in—images of the ways she could show Matt some appreciation, and ways he might show her.

"Problem?" asked Clay.

She pulled herself together. "Only with the thought of going easy on Matt. You know what he's like; you give him an inch, and he'll take a mile. I admit, he saved us some hassle by bringing West in, and I thanked him. That's enough if you ask me."

"Whatever you say. You're the one in charge here."

She smiled. She was. But only because he'd put her in charge. "That's right, and I need to get on with it. I missed this morning already. So, is there anything I can do for you? How long are you here for?"

"I don't need anything. I just wanted to come see your face while we're in town. Marianne's having coffee with Shawnee, so I thought I'd come see if you had anything to tell me about."

He held her gaze again, and she wondered if he really did know about last night. "Nope. It sounds like you're as up to date as I am on Matt's situation. I spoke to Carson on Saturday. He's doing well. I think this tour was a great idea for him. Opening for Lee is giving him insight into how a major tour works. He's loving it, and he's learning a lot. When he gets back, I want to get him in the studio."

Clay smiled. "I think that's a great idea. He's building a decent following. Lee thinks he's a great kid and mentioned doing a single with him. I was thinking I could do the same."

Autumn grinned. "That's fantastic. Have you been reading my notes? I planned to ask both of you if you'd be willing to work with him. If we can launch his album with singles from you two on there, it'll broaden his appeal. His appeal with the younger crowd is undeniable and he also has the old school sound. If we can pair that with an obvious endorsement and collaboration with you and Lee, it'll bring in the older generation and give him a pretty universal appeal. He's going to be big."

"I believe he is. I'm excited about the kid's future."

Autumn smiled. "Me too. Anyway, you didn't answer my question; how long are you here for?"

"I didn't answer, because I don't know yet. I'll get my orders from Marianne when she and Shawnee get done."

Autumn laughed. "I doubt Marianne has ever given you an order in all the time you've been together. She's too sweet. I should give her lessons."

Clay shook his head rapidly. "She is the sweetest person I've ever known, and don't you dare go teaching her your ways. I'd be doomed."

"I think you're safe. She doesn't have it in her to boss you around. It's not her style; she gets her way by being such a lovely person that you—and the rest of us—want to do whatever she wants."

Autumn loved the way he nodded. There was no question that he was a man in love and would do anything for his fiancée. "That's right; she is one amazing lady, and I cannot wait to make her my wife."

Autumn leaned forward eagerly. "Have the two of you set a date then?"

He sighed. "Not yet, but we're getting closer."

"I hope it's soon."

"So do I. So do I." He pushed his chair back and got to his feet. "I'll get out of your hair. I know you need to play catch-up. I'll let you know if we're staying; you should come over for dinner if we are. You and Matt."

She pursed her lips, and he chuckled. "How many years have I been telling you that you should give him a chance?"

She had to believe that he didn't know about last night. He was right. He did tell her all the time that she should give Matt a chance. This wasn't anything out of the ordinary. It just felt that way, because she was finally considering it as a possibility. "Let me know what your plans are."

She stared at the door after he closed it behind him. Was she really considering the possibility? She blew out a sigh—or should she firmly close the door on it?

Chapter Eight

Matt sat in the reception area outside Corbin's office. He swung his legs over the arm of the chair and leafed through a magazine. He'd brought West over here. It was the least he could do. West was about to become one of the people he spent most of his time with, and the guy didn't even have a place to stay yet. He didn't seem perturbed by that fact at all. He said he had plenty of places he could crash. Still, Matt felt responsible for him. He'd offered him his spare room until he found his feet, and even though West had insisted that wouldn't take him long, Matt couldn't help regretting it.

He wasn't the kind of guy to just leave West to his own devices. Sure, he was a grown man, and he had plenty of connections here in town. Nonetheless, Matt saw it as his duty. It was just what a decent guy did, as far as he was concerned. Even if it meant that he wouldn't be able to invite Autumn over to his place. He blew out a sigh. Who knew if she'd come anyway? Maybe that was part of it? Maybe subconsciously, he knew that she was going to blow him off again—that she'd decided that their close call last night was as close as she wanted to get—and if he couldn't invite her over then he wouldn't force her to tell him her decision.

He swung his legs down to the floor. It wasn't like him to be so pessimistic. Nope. If he'd had a close call like that with any other woman, he'd be eagerly anticipating the reward when he closed the deal—confident in the knowledge that that day, or more likely night, would be coming very soon.

But Autumn wasn't like any other woman. She was different. Unique. He sighed again. Special. She was special, all right.

He looked up when Corbin's door opened, and he and West appeared. They shook hands and then Corbin smiled at Matt. "We're all set here. You guys can get back to work."

"That's great, thanks."

"Are you back in the studio this afternoon?"

"No. I canceled today's session when I heard about Reggie. I thought it'd take us a while to find someone."

"And then this guy landed in your lap." He grasped West's shoulder. "It's good to have you back in town, and even better to know that we get to work with you."

"It's good to be back. I'm looking forward to working with you both." He nodded at Matt. "Should we go see the other guys? I'd like to touch base with them. Make sure they're okay with me coming on board."

"Sure." Matt had been half hoping that he could drop Weston off at his apartment and then go into the office and see Autumn. It was only a half-baked idea, though. Autumn would probably be too busy to see him even if she wanted to. And it did make sense to get West together with the rest of the band.

"I'll stop by the studio tomorrow," said Corbin.

"Great, we'll see you then," said Matt.

Corbin held his gaze for a moment. "And you're sure Autumn's okay with all of this?"

"Yep. I'd go as far as to say she's happy about it. But you're the one who has to iron out the details. She'll be expecting your call."

"I plan to call her just as soon as you leave. I'm just asking if there's anything I should be aware of when I do."

West gave Matt a puzzled look, but he just shrugged and asked. "Like what?"

"I was hoping you'd tell me. Have you pissed her off lately? Any spats I should know about? You have to bear in mind that I usually take the brunt of it when you roil her up."

Matt pursed his lips. He tried to imagine the look on his manager's face if he told him that last night, he'd had her pinned underneath him on the sofa, her legs wrapped around his back, moaning into his mouth as he kissed her. You could say she'd been pretty roiled up then. He sucked in a sharp breath. Nope. He was hardly going to go there, though the ache in his pants told him how much he wished he was still there.

"You're safe," he told Corbin with a smile. "I didn't piss her off this weekend." Well, maybe that wasn't true, but he had managed to smooth things over—and more—before they'd left Seattle. "In fact, I think we came back on better terms than we've been for a while."

Corbin raised an eyebrow. "Okay, well, you two get out of here then. I'm going to call her now before you manage to annoy her again somehow."

"Okay. See you tomorrow."

As they walked back across the parking lot to Matt's truck, West shot him a sly look.

"What?"

West grinned. "I'm curious about something, but I'm not sure I should ask."

"Ask away," said Matt. "I'm an open book."

"Are you really?"

"I sure am." They reached the truck and climbed in before West spoke again.

Matt was buckling his seat belt, but the buckle slipped out of his fingers and shot back up to his shoulder when he heard West's question.

"How long have you been doing her?"

He turned to look at his new drummer. "What?!"

West chuckled. "You heard me, and I'm right, aren't I? The tension between the two of you was obvious from the minute I showed up this morning. Did you guys have a fight?"

Matt blew out a sigh. "We're always having some kind of fight, but it's not how it seems. That's just the way we work together. I'm not *doing* her, as you so eloquently put it."

West held up a hand. "Sorry. I didn't mean to be crass about it. I just figured … you know … that's the way it goes, isn't it?"

Matt shrugged. "I guess so. In the industry. Yeah. It probably is. But that's not the way it's going with Autumn and me."

West grinned. "But you wish it was? Is that why Corbin said you wind her up and piss her off?"

"I suppose so. We have …" Matt thought about it. He'd been about to say that they had a long and complicated history. But, if he was honest, there was nothing complicated about it. It was simple. He'd wanted to get with Autumn ever since he'd started working with her. She, on the other hand, wanted nothing to do with him. Or, at least, she hadn't until last night. And maybe she didn't again now.

West was watching his face. "Should I finish that sentence for you? You have the hots for each other? You have major sexual chemistry going on? You have a very limited amount of time left that you can hold out before you screw each other's brains out?"

Matt had to laugh. "All of the above, I guess. But none of those were going to be my answer. What I was going to say is that we have a complicated situation. I've had a thing for her for years. She's blown me off for years. I'm starting to think I might finally get somewhere. But all her reasons for not getting involved with me are still valid. She told me I should think about them, too."

"She sounds smart enough to me. What would happen afterward?"

Matt rolled his eyes. He'd bared his heart to Autumn when he'd said what if they were to get together and there were no afterward. He didn't feel like saying the same thing to West. He'd sound like a sap, to a guy who was known for making the most of the benefits of his position—and who'd thought it was okay to ask if Matt was *doing* Autumn. "I think we could be adult enough about it."

West nodded. "Well, good luck is all I have to say. I remember when Summer was still here. Everyone had the hots for her, but I always thought Autumn was the more attractive of them. Don't get me wrong, Summer's a stunner, but Autumn is, too, and there's something more to her—an edge, a hint of danger." He laughed. "Don't worry. I've not got my sights on her. She's too much of a tough nut for my taste. All I'm saying is, I can see the appeal."

Matt fastened his seat belt and started the truck. He'd rather close the subject and move on. "What is your taste? I seem to remember you weren't too discerning when you were here before."

West laughed. "Guilty as charged. I was terrible. But I've changed while I've been gone." He shrugged. "I wouldn't say I have a physical taste anymore. I'm attracted to a kind of person."

Matt raised an eyebrow at him before he pulled out of the parking lot. "I'm not sure if you're winding me up here. I'm half expecting the punchline to come and you're going to say—strippers."

West laughed. "No. Not anymore. I've come to appreciate women's spirit."

Matt made a face. "Did you go all new age-y down in Central America?"

"No. Not in so many words anyway. I just got to see a different take on life. I met people with different experiences. People who've fought all kinds of battles and come out the other side stronger and better. I think, now, I'm attracted to women who've faced their demons or their weakness or their burdens—their challenges, I guess—and who've come out the other side stronger and more, I dunno … humble." He laughed self-consciously. "I know that probably sounds like a crock of shit, but I know what I mean."

"No, I think I understand."

West laughed again. "Do you think you could explain it to me then?"

"I do. It sounds to me like you're attracted to real women who know how to handle their shit, while before, you were interested in girls who made out they didn't have any shit."

"That's it. You nailed it."

Matt smiled. "You might have to start fishing in different ponds than you used to. Our line of work attracts more of the girls than the real women."

West nodded. "I'm fully aware of that. It was part of the reason I left. I need to be more careful this time around. I have to be upfront with you, too, Matt."

Matt shot a glance over at him. "About what?"

"I want to be back here for good this time. I've got a handle on myself. Got my head on straight. But if I start to get off-track again, go down that same old road, I'm going to have to leave. I missed the music. I missed the industry, and I don't think that old way of life will drag me back in, but if it does …"

Matt smiled as he turned into the parking lot under his building. "That's okay. I get it. I don't think you'll have too much of a problem staying on the straight and narrow. We have a good group of friends—real people, down to earth, tell-it-to-you-like-it-is friends. If you let them know what you're trying to do, they'll help keep you on track. I can be the little angel on your shoulder if you want me to be, and Lance will give you shit if you start putting play before work anyway. Levi … well, Levi's a different story. If you fall in with him, you two could lead each other astray, but …"

"Good to know. So, I should hang out with Lance and be wary of Levi."

"Wary is a strong word. Aware might be better. He's a great guy. You'll love him. Everybody does, but it's easy to get sucked into the good times when Levi's around."

"Thanks and noted."

"Come on then." Matt pulled the truck into his space and got out. "I thought you'd want to dump your bag and maybe take a shower, so I texted the guys while you were in with Corbin. They're meeting us here. I'd already given up this afternoon's studio time before I knew you were on board or we could have met there."

"This might be better. I can get to know them as people a little before I get to know them as musicians."

"True." Matt made his way to the elevators and West followed. "I think you'll get along great with them."

When Autumn finally made it home to her apartment, she took her bag through to the laundry room and set a load going before putting away her toiletries. She kept a travel sized set of everything ready to go. And she restocked the little shampoo bottle and the other liquids before she finished putting everything away. Once her bag was back in its place in the closet, she went through to the kitchen and poured herself a glass of wine.

She pulled up a seat at the counter and started to flip through her mail. There was nothing urgent or even interesting. She went and opened the fridge door wondering if there was anything in there she might feel like cooking or if she should order take out. The mostly bare shelves reminded her that she hadn't been to the grocery store in weeks and told her that it was looking like a pizza delivery kind of night. She closed the door with a sigh and picked up her phone to call in her order.

When she hung up, she went to stand in front of the windows to look out at the city. She loved the view from this place. The city spread out before her, and she could see all the familiar landmarks. She'd bought this place to celebrate her first anniversary of head of McAdam Records. It was one of the most expensive buildings in town. Her neighbors included some of country music's biggest names and some of its lesser-known names who held much of the power. Looking to her right, she could see Matt's building. She took a sip of her wine. So, she shouldn't look right. She needed to have a serious talk with herself about Matt. She needed to get clear on what she was doing before she let her mind—especially her imagination—start to run through scenarios of what she and Matt could do—what they could have done last night, and, in all honesty, could be doing again tonight if she hadn't put the brakes on.

She wondered if he was in his apartment right now. Probably not. He'd taken West to see Corbin this afternoon. And when she'd talked to Corbin, he'd told her that he was taking him to meet up with the rest of the band. They were probably out on the town by now. She chewed the inside of her lip. She knew what they were like. There'd be women hitting on them. Levi would take them up on it. Lance would play along for a while and then get bored and go home. Matt would be the center of the party and make all the girls feel special. That was what he did. He made women feel special. It was a knack he had. Was that all he'd done with her last night? She didn't think so, but she wasn't sure. Not sure enough to trust him enough to finally let her guard down. It was ironic in a way that she'd only stopped things because she knew she was drunk and her fail safes had kicked in. If she'd been sober, she probably would have gone through with it.

When her pizza arrived, she poured herself a fresh glass of wine and went to settle on the sofa. She turned the TV on and flicked through the channels while she munched.

She hit mute when the phone rang and picked it up to see whether she wanted to answer. It wasn't Matt, and it was only when she saw her sister's name on the display that she realized how much she'd wanted it to be him.

"Hey, Summer."

"Hey, sis. Did you get back okay?"

"Yeah. I texted you last night, remember?"

"Only to tell me that you were in Seattle. I thought you'd let me know when you made it home."

Autumn laughed. "Yep. I'm home safe and sound. Sorry that I didn't check in with you."

"That's okay. You know I worry, so I had to make sure. How was your night in Seattle?"

Autumn pursed her lips. She was getting paranoid. Her mind immediately jumped to the possibility that Matt might have told her about last night. But that was crazy. Why would he?

"It was good. Productive, at least. I told you in the text that we were going to meet with West this morning? Well, it worked out even better than that. He was ready to come back here, so he flew back with us and went to see Corbin with Matt today. I talked to Corbin this afternoon, and we should be all set to sign the contracts tomorrow."

"That's awesome. I like West, and he's super talented."

"He is, and he's a good guy."

"And what about the other good guy?"

"Who's that?" Autumn usually got irritated when Summer teased her about Matt, but tonight she wondered whether she might ask her sister's advice.

Summer laughed. "You know full well who I mean. Matt. Did the two of you make the most of your evening in Seattle together?"

Autumn bit the inside of her lip.

"Well? Don't tell me you're mad at him again. What did he do this time?"

"Nothing." Autumn took a deep breath. She needed to talk to someone about what was or wasn't or might be going on between her and Matt. "But I'll bet you can guess what he was about to do till I stopped him at the last minute."

The line was quiet for a long moment until Summer squealed. "Oh. My. Gosh! What happened? How did you …? And why didn't you …?"

Autumn had to laugh. "We called a truce on our usual crap and went out for dinner. It was a nice time. He was good company. We went back for a drink afterward and we almost …"

"I can't believe it! That's awesome, Autumn!"

"What's awesome? That we almost did or that we didn't?"

"That you almost did! The poor guy's been in love with you for years—"

"Ha! Don't be crazy, Summer. He's always claimed to have a thing for me. I wasn't sure I believed that, at least, not beyond the fact that I'm a female with a pulse. Don't you go pulling your little hopeless romantic thing and turn it into something else."

"It is something else, Autumn. He's in love with you. It's not just me. He is. I can't believe he didn't tell you he has feelings for you."

Autumn's heart was racing. "He did, but that's just what he does. Tell a woman what she wants to hear; tell her anything that will get her panties around her ankles."

"That's not true! He used to be like that. I should know. I toured with him when he first started out, and he was as bad as the rest of them, maybe worse. But he's changed, sis. He's changed since he met you. Tell me you weren't mean to him?"

"I wasn't mean."

"So, why did you stop him at the last minute?"

"Summer! Stopping a man at the last minute isn't mean!"

"I know. I didn't mean it that way. I mean ... what happened?"

"I told him I didn't want to."

"Oh." Her sister sounded so disappointed she felt bad.

"I told him that I'd need to wrap my head around it first."

"Yay!" Summer squealed. "When you do wrap your head around it, you'll see how perfect this is."

"I think I'm more likely to conclude that it's a bad idea."

"Oh, don't do that. Please! In fact, promise me you'll give it a go? I know you two are made for each other. I just know it."

Autumn laughed. "You're such a hopeless little romantic."

"Maybe. But humor me on this one, would you? I think I can help you out here. You want to sleep with him, don't you?"

Autumn nodded but didn't speak.

"It's okay; you don't need to admit it out loud—we both know you do. So, you can tell yourself that you're just giving him a shot because I badgered you into it. You can sleep with him—like you've wanted to for years, and tell yourself whatever you like, but I know—I just know—that once the two of you get together, that'll be it. You'll stay together and end up together, and I will be sooo happy."

Autumn laughed. "And what if it all goes horribly wrong, and I still have to work with him?"

"Then you'll figure it out. You're fiery. He's a handful, but you both care enough about your careers and about Clay to let anything become too much of a problem."

Autumn tried to hold in a smile. Her sister had just given her the out she'd been looking for. She was right, both she and Matt adored Clay and felt like they owed him everything. If things didn't work out, if they got ugly, she knew that their shared love of Clay would mean neither of them would do anything to hurt the label.

"Say something?"

"Thanks."

"Oooh!" Summer squealed again. "Are you going to give him a chance then?"

"I do believe I am."

Chapter Nine

"Damn, that sounded great!" exclaimed Lance.

"Don't sound so surprised," said Levi. "I told you it would."

Lance nodded grudgingly. "You know I like to be the ideas guy when it comes to production. Your role is to look pretty. But I've got to hand it to you, those harmonies and closing out on the acoustic … wow! It's amazing."

Matt grinned at them. It really did sound great. They'd been working all morning on one of the last tracks for the album. West had fitted right in with the others. He was super talented. Matt had had no worries there, but he wasn't sure how well he'd gel with the other guys. He was fitting in better than Reggie ever had. Reggie was a great guy and they all had a lot of respect for him, but he was that bit older, and he was—understandably—more concerned about his family than about joking around and hanging out with the guys. West, on the other hand, acted like they were his family. He'd invited them all out for dinner on his first night here. It'd been a great bonding session for them as a band—even if Matt had spent half the time wishing that he was with Autumn instead.

He hadn't seen her or heard from her since they got back from Seattle. He'd had his phone in his hand ready to text her at least a dozen times a day every day since. But he talked himself out of it each time. She'd told him she needed time to think about it. Left to his own devices, he'd rather persuade her than wait for her, but he was trying to respect her wishes in the hopes that would show her how serious he was about her—about them.

"I have another idea, about 'Red Dirt,'" said Levi.

They all looked at him. "Yeah. I thought we should bring the girls in on the chorus. Make it big and kind of anthemy."

Matt thought about it. He could see that working. 'Red Dirt' was the kind of song that had the potential to become a summertime, feel-good anthem. He nodded slowly and looked at the others. "I like it. What do you guys think?"

Lance rolled his eyes. "I think Levi just wants to get some women in here. He's gone without for almost a whole week now."

Levi punched his arm. "You might be partially right there, but come on, you have to admit it'd sound good."

"Yeah. Much as I don't want to admit it, you're right. Who are you thinking of bringing in, though? Jan and Alexa are out of town."

Matt knew Levi had ulterior motives when his eyes lit up. "Well, I was talking to these two chicks last night at Laurie's place and—"

"And let me guess, you told them you could make them famous?" Lance didn't look impressed.

"No." Levi shook his head. "Have a little faith, would you? I know I'm a player, but I don't mix business with pleasure."

Matt nodded to himself; that was true. Levi might have no qualms about sleeping with members of the audience, but to Matt's knowledge, he'd never slept with one of the singers or musicians they'd brought in, and there had been plenty of them over the last few years.

"So, what makes you think they'd be right for this?" he asked.

Levi turned to him. "I heard them sing harmonies. They're freaking amazing. It's a different sound. They're fresh in town. They came from Arizona—they have some connection to Laurie somehow. I dunno, I didn't pay too much attention to that bit. But you need to hear them, Matt."

"Are they going to be there tonight?" If he knew Levi, they would be.

Levi grinned. "I told them I might bring the rest of the band in, and that if you guys like their sound ..."

West finally spoke up. "If us guys like it?" He looked around at them. "I'm just learning the ropes here. I'm guessing it's Matt's decision, right? Or Autumn's? But we get to have our say? Have some input?"

"You sure do," said Matt. "The contracts are set up so that we're all separate, but as far as I'm concerned, we're a band, a team. We all contribute as much as each other, in different ways. I supply the lead vocals. Levi is bass and good looks. Lance is lead guitar and production genius. And you? Well, so far we know that you're drums, and the rest we'll learn with time."

West smiled. "I guess we will. If I had to tell you right now what I can bring to the table, I'm a pretty good motivator. I know how to keep the mood light when things are going down, and I know how to keep everyone working till we reach our goals."

The others nodded at Matt. It seemed they liked that idea as much as he did. Reggie was a great guy, but it sometimes felt like he brought a dark cloud into the room with him and brought everyone's mood down. If West could keep their spirits up, then he'd be an even more welcome addition.

"That sounds good to me," said Levi. "So how about you motivate these two into coming to Laurie's tonight to hear the girls—and we may as well have dinner and knock a few back while we're there, right?"

They all nodded their agreement. Matt had been considering whether tonight would be the night that he called Autumn. But a night out with the guys would be good for the band, and it would force him to stick with being patient.

~ ~ ~

Autumn looked up and checked the clock on the wall. It was only four o'clock, but she was thinking of calling it a day. It wasn't like her to leave early, but she hadn't been able to concentrate all afternoon. Her mind kept drifting—drifting to Matt and to Seattle, to the way he'd made her feel on that sofa. She felt her nipples stiffen at the memory. She'd been kicking herself all week for telling him to stop. She wished she'd just let things run their natural course. She sat up straight. But she hadn't. There was no point crying over spilt milk. She'd decided in the moment that they'd do better to wait until she was sober. Now she was sober, she'd had a few days to think about it. She'd second-guessed herself a bunch, but she always came back to the conclusion that yes, she wanted to sleep with him. She wanted to see how a relationship between them might work, too. But that seemed like too big of an ask. Sleeping with him would be a start—if it was an end, too, then so be it. If it was a beginning, they could see where things went from there.

She made a face when her phone rang. She should have left while she was thinking about it. Now she'd no doubt be here for hours dealing with whatever problem was about to land in her lap.

"This is Autumn," she answered.

"Hi, Autumn. This is Paige. In accounts."

"What's up, Paige?" She wanted to remind her that she didn't need to tell her she was in accounts every time they spoke. Autumn knew who she was, where she worked, and just how lucky they were to have her. The girl was brilliant. She wasn't just *in* accounts; she'd stepped up as the company accountant when Griff had retired last year. And as much as Autumn had loved Griff, Paige made him seem like a dinosaur—in his methods and his results.

"I, umm. I wondered if …"

Autumn deliberately calmed herself and got a grip on her impatience. She had no time for people who mumbled. She preferred to deal with go-getters than shrinking violets. She made an exception in Paige's case, though. Paige might be what you would call socially awkward, but she was also undeniably brilliant. Autumn had discovered that if you gave her the time to say things her own way, and the confidence that she wouldn't be ridiculed for saying them, she'd reward you with either business insights that saved thousands, innovative ideas that made the label run more efficiently, or more and more lately, insightful comments about artists or execs and hilarious one-liners. Autumn made herself breathe in and out slowly and evenly while she waited.

"I wondered if …"

Autumn couldn't help herself. "I'll tell you what. Would it be easier to tell me in person? I could come down there?"

"Umm. Only if … if it's not an inconvenience?"

"Nope. It'll do me good to get out of my office. I'll be down there in a few." She grabbed her purse and shut down her computer. Hopefully, she'd be stopping to see Paige on her way out; if it turned out there was a problem that she needed to stick around to deal with, then she could always come back up here.

When the elevator doors opened, she smiled at the sight of Bianca, the head of PR standing there waiting.

"Hey. Are you sneaking out early?"

Bianca laughed, looking a little guilty. "You caught me. It's just one of those days, and I hit a natural break-off point and thought, you know what …? But I can stay if you need me."

"Hell, no. Get out of here. There must be something in the air today. I was planning to do the same thing myself."

"Do you have plans, or do you want to play hooky together? I'm considering taking myself over to Laurie's. You should come. Then we can pretend that we're talking business, and I won't feel so guilty about taking off early."

Autumn considered it. "I'd like to, but I'm just on my way to see Paige. She needs to tell me something."

"Ah, that might take a while."

Autumn smiled. "It might. She's getting better, though. Maybe I should invite her; that might help her open up a little."

"You can try. I ask her to come out all the time, but she turns me down. Maybe she'll say yes since you're the boss. I think she considers me to be too frivolous since I'm just the PR lady."

Autumn had to laugh at that. "If she considers you to be frivolous, then she doesn't know you very well, does she?" Bianca was driven, to say the least. Autumn admired that about her; they had a lot in common.

The elevator doors closed behind Autumn, and Bianca made a face. "I guess that's my decision made, then. I'm waiting here for you and Paige. But if she doesn't want to come, or you're going to be a while, let me know? I'll meet you there."

"Give me five minutes, and I'll let you know either way."

"Okay."

Bianca went back into her office, and Autumn made her way down the hall to Paige's office and tapped sharply on the door.

"Come in!" The way Paige said it, Autumn half expected her to add, *I surrender!*

"Hey. Before we start, is this something we need to be in the office to discuss?"

Paige considered the question then shook her head.

"Okay, and is it confidential or would you mind if Bianca hears what you have to say?"

Paige's eyebrows knit together, then she slowly shook her head again. "It's not confidential. However, I should tell you that it might take me a little longer to explain with Bianca present."

Autumn raised an eyebrow. "Because you're uncomfortable with her?"

"Not with her. Just with speaking in front of people."

Autumn nodded. "Then we should take care of this here and now. I was asking because we're going to go to Laurie's Tavern. I thought you might like to come, and we could kill two birds with one stone."

Paige held her gaze for a long moment. "I'd like to come. If you don't mind dealing with my awkwardness, then I think I should make the effort. I'm attempting to accept all the opportunities that come my way." She gave a faint smile. "I need to expand my comfort zone. It is, admittedly, rather small."

Autumn smiled and reached out to touch her arm, though she immediately regretted doing so when she saw the look on Paige's face. "Sorry."

"Don't be. I understand that physical touch is an expression of support and encouragement. I appreciate the sentiment."

"If not the act itself," Autumn finished for her.

Paige gave her a sheepish smile. "I'm getting better."

"You are. There was a time not so long ago I would never have dared to come down here and talk to you. I knew it'd freak you out."

"It would have. Now, I'm not even freaked out by you extending a social invitation. I'm accepting with only a little trepidation."

Autumn chuckled. "I hope you'll enjoy it, but if you don't, feel free to say so and leave—or just leave and say so later if that's easier on you."

"Thanks. I know some people find your direct manner to be harsh. I find it reassuring because I know that I don't have to decipher social niceties with you."

Autumn laughed. "I'm going to take that as a compliment." Though she had to wonder who had told Paige she was harsh. There was no way Paige had figured it out for herself.

"That's what I intended. What time are we leaving?"

"Now."

"Oh." Paige looked around her office.

"Does that work for you? We can meet you there if you prefer?"

A look of relief crossed Paige's face. "That would be better. I'll be there shortly."

Autumn went back to the elevators and stuck her head in the PR office on the way by. "Bianca. Are you coming?"

Several heads turned in her direction, no doubt wondering if Bianca was in trouble to be summoned like that. Autumn smiled to herself as she waited by the elevator. She might as well keep up her harsh reputation.

Chapter Ten

Autumn rode with Bianca over to Laurie's Tavern. There was no point in both of them battling traffic. When they arrived, Autumn pushed the door open and let Bianca go in ahead of her.

Just a few steps inside, Bianca stopped dead, and Autumn walked straight into the back of her. "What the …?"

"Sorry. But look who's here. Do you want to stay?"

Autumn looked over her shoulder, and her stomach turned a somersault when she saw Matt and the rest of the band sitting at the end of the bar. She balled her fists, surprised by how sweaty her palms felt all of a sudden. Her mind raced, scenes of her and Matt's night in Seattle raced before her eyes. His voice filled her head. *If you think I'm not interested in you that way, then you're dumber than a box of rocks, baby girl.*

She looked at Bianca—Bianca had no idea what had happened between them in Seattle, so why was she suggesting that Autumn might want to leave?

"Speak up now if you do. Otherwise, we won't get our girly drink after work. We'll have to listen to the egos and the bullshit, and no doubt end up talking work the whole time."

Autumn sucked in a deep breath and nodded slowly. "Can you stand it, or would you rather go somewhere else?"

Bianca made a face. "You don't need to ask. Lance is with them. You know I will endure no end of bullshit and ego from the others just so I can sit and stare at his pretty face." She gave a mock sigh. "And his ass, and his shoulders and ..."

Autumn chuckled. "Ah. Of course. In that case, I guess we're staying."

As they started to make their way to the bar, West turned and spotted them. Autumn was surprised that instead of greeting them or even acknowledging them in any way, he dug Matt in the ribs and leaned in to say something to him and then laughed.

Autumn's blood ran cold. Had Matt told him? Were they laughing about the fact that Matt had almost made it into her panties? She pressed her lips together. She hoped not—for their sake.

"Ladies!" Levi was the first to greet them. He slid down from his stool and came to wrap Bianca in a hug. When she managed to wriggle free, he met Autumn's gaze. He knew better than to try to hug on her. Instead, he caught her hand and lifted it to his lips.

"Greetings, illustrious leader. To what do we owe the pleasure of your company?"

Autumn laughed. "To the fact that we didn't know you'd be here. We'd have gone elsewhere otherwise."

Lance looked concerned, which wasn't unusual for him. He was the most serious of Matt's guys. "We're almost done with the last few tracks, and we traded out studio time with Vince. We're not wasting it."

Autumn smiled. "No need to explain. I trust your judgment." As she spoke those words, she finally turned to look at Matt.

He met her gaze and smiled his most genuine smile. It set her heart fluttering madly against her ribcage. "I'm glad to hear it. If you don't know you can trust me to do the right thing by now …"

She gave him a brief nod. Point taken.

Levi slung his arm around Bianca's shoulders. "So, what can I get you, ladies?"

"How about an introduction first?" asked Bianca.

Autumn didn't miss the way Lance's face fell as Levi introduced her to West. Bianca claimed that Lance didn't even notice she was alive, but that evidently wasn't true. He was noticing her right now. And by the look on his face, he didn't like the way that West was noticing her, too.

"Autumn Breese! I hope you're not here to drag these reprobates back to work. I told them I wouldn't harbor them as fugitives, but they promised me that their work was done for the day."

Autumn grinned at Laurie, the owner of the bar. "It's fine. I can't complain about them knocking off early and finding their way here. Bianca and I did the same thing."

"Awesome. What can I get you, then? It's on the house."

"I'll take a beer, thanks, Laurie," said Bianca. "I could use one after the day I've had."

"Coming right up. Same for you, Autumn?"

She shook her head. "No. I'll take an iced tea for now. I still have some business to take care of first."

She felt rather than saw Matt's head swing toward her when she said that. Did he think she meant business with him?

"What kind of business?" asked Levi. You could always rely on him to ask the question.

"Paige is coming to join us."

His eyes widened in shock. "Paige is coming out for a drink?"

"We have a few details to go over, and yeah, she's going to join us for a drink afterward. So, take it easy on her, would you? This is a big step for her."

Levi nodded rapidly. "I won't say a word. I won't tease. I won't joke. I won't flirt."

Autumn laughed. "Good boy. What's up, does she scare you?"

Lance laughed. "You don't know?"

Autumn raised an eyebrow. "Know what?"

"That he's totally besotted with her!"

Autumn laughed out loud at that. "You've got to be kidding me?"

Lance shook his head solemnly. "Our Levi, resident manwhore, is so totally enamored with the company accountant that he has been known to declare that he'd give up all his wicked ways if she would just give him the time of day."

Matt chuckled. "To be fair, that was after a heavy night's drinking."

"Maybe so," said Levi. "But I still stand by it now I'm sober." He held up his glass of orange juice. "I do solemnly declare that … oh." He lowered his glass and dropped his gaze to the floor. "She's here!" He whispered so loudly that Paige probably heard him from the spot where she stood by the front door.

She was scanning the room as if searching for Autumn, but she could hardly miss her. It wasn't even five o'clock yet, and the place was nowhere near full.

"I'll go and finish off with her." Autumn looked at Bianca. "I assume you'd rather hang with these guys?"

Bianca nodded and lifted her beer. "Yep. I can wait till you're done."

~ ~ ~

As Matt watched Autumn walk over to join Paige, he shifted uncomfortably in his seat. He usually got a little buzz whenever she was around. But the memory of their near miss in Seattle now had him dealing with a full-on boner. Her ass seemed to taunt him as she walked away. Damn! He needed to get a grip. He brought his bottle to his mouth but stopped with it halfway there when West caught his gaze and raised an eyebrow. Matt shook his head and took a slug of his beer.

"So, how's the album coming?" asked Bianca.

"Not as hard as you would be if I—" Levi started with a grin, but Lance cut him short as he shoved his shoulder.

"Don't!" He blew out a sigh and gave Bianca an apologetic smile. "I'm sorry; we can't take him anywhere. At least, not in decent company."

Bianca smiled back at him. "That's okay. I'm used to him."

"Maybe, but going back to your question, the album's coming along great. We should be done soon, right, Matt?"

Matt nodded. "Yeah. Just a few more songs left to record."

"And here come the ladies who are going to help us lay them down." Levi jerked his head to where two girls had just come in.

"Hot damn!" exclaimed West.

Matt couldn't help nodding his head in agreement. The blonde was a stunner. Long hair, perfect pink pouty lips. A rack that … He cast a guilty glance toward Autumn. Hell. Just because you owned a Jaguar didn't mean you wouldn't look when a Porsche went by. He didn't feel any attraction to the blonde. But he wasn't blind either. She was one of those women who would turn heads wherever she went.

Lance gave Levi a stern look. "You remember telling us earlier that you don't mix business and pleasure, right?"

"Well, if that's a band rule, I vote that we find different singers," said West.

Lance chuckled. "I don't know you too well yet, but I have to warn you that you might be setting yourself up for disappointment. The ladies can't seem to resist Levi. I don't think you'll get a look in."

West smiled. "I don't think it'll be an issue—unless you want them both, Levi?"

Levi shook his head. "Nope. I'm true to my word. My interest in them is purely professional. The only blonde that's got my attention in here is sitting with Autumn."

Matt made a face. "You're joking, right?"

He shook his head solemnly. "I'm deadly serious. Look at her!"

Matt did. Paige was a good-looking woman. She, too, had long blonde hair, and he noticed for the first time that she also had a rather appealing figure, but still. He found it hard to believe that Levi appreciated it. She was hardly his usual type. And Matt couldn't believe that she could still hold his attention over the stunning blonde who'd just walked in.

Bianca slapped Levi's arm. "I hope you're not being mean? She's a bit awkward, but she's really nice."

Levi ran his hand through his hair and looked up at the ceiling in frustration. "Why won't they believe me?" he asked the lazily turning fan above his head.

Lance looked around at them. "Strange as it seems, I can vouch for the fact that he is totally serious. He has a thing for the accountant."

"Wow." Matt shook his head and turned to look at West. "And by your comment about him not wanting both, does that mean that you like the other one?"

West grinned. "Like is such a weak little word." He slapped Levi's shoulder. "I'd appreciate an introduction."

Levi grinned at him and slid down from his stool. "Come with me, my friend."

Matt watched them approach the two girls.

"Oh, my God! Did you see that?" asked Bianca.

Matt nodded. "It looks like Levi isn't the one we need to worry about."

"I swear I just saw an electric current arc between West and the other girl," said Bianca.

Lance sighed. "So, there's probably no point even hearing them sing, right? We can't work with them if he's going to go there."

Matt shook his head. "I think West has a little more self-restraint than Levi. It could still work."

Lance nodded. "I hope so."

Autumn smiled at Paige. "Thanks for doing all of this. You're going to save us thousands every week, just with this one idea."

Paige nodded. "That's my job."

"Okay, well, I'll sign whatever you need me to when we're back in the office tomorrow, and you can get it rolling."

"Excellent."

"And are you comfortable to come and join the others?"

Paige shot a glance over to where Matt was sitting at the bar with Bianca and Lance. A quick glance told Autumn that Levi and West had already found themselves a pair of hotties. She hoped that West wasn't going to turn into Levi's hunting partner. It was tough enough to keep one of them out of trouble.

"This might sound like a strange request, but would you mind if I observe the interactions for a few minutes before we go over? I like to get a read on a situation before I have to deal with it."

"Sure thing. And don't you believe that it's a strange request. I think we all like to do that when we can. It's just that most people would never admit it."

Paige looked surprised. "You think it's normal?"

Autumn nodded. "I think a lot of your reactions are very normal. You're perceived as not-so-normal only because your need to do things your way is stronger than the need to bow to the social expectations that rule most people's lives."

Paige nodded and turned her attention to the group at the bar.

Autumn watched Levi and West bring the girls over to join them. She did that partly because she was trying not to just stare at Matt and partly because she wanted to get a read on West. To her surprise, he wasn't tripping over his tongue around the stunning blonde. He seemed far more interested in her dark-haired, dark-skinned companion.

When she did sneak a peek at Matt, her heart sank. *He* was looking at the blonde like he wanted to eat her up. She pressed her lips together. What did she expect? He didn't owe her a damned thing. Any man would ogle that girl; even Autumn couldn't help but stare. She was what you'd call drop-dead gorgeous.

Paige turned to her. "Will you tell me if I have this right?"

"What's that?"

"Bianca and Lance are each trying to hide the fact that they like each other. Weston is rather taken with the Hispanic-looking girl. Levi, rather surprisingly, is not as interested in the pretty one as he's making out. Am I right?"

Autumn smiled. "Absolutely spot on. You're very insightful. You just need to learn to trust your instincts."

Paige shook her head. "My instincts are flawed. A fifty-fifty accuracy rate is no better than chance."

Autumn gave her a puzzled look. "Your math is never wrong, so it must be mine that's off. I'd say you were one hundred percent accurate. What did I miss?"

Paige lowered her glasses to the end of her nose and peered over them at her. "You only missed what I didn't say. I thought it prudent not to mention that it appears to me that Matt is more interested in what you're doing over here than in either of the new arrivals."

That made Autumn smile. She'd been feeling a twinge of jealousy over the way he was looking at that blonde.

"And ..." Autumn was surprised to see a touch of color in Paige's cheeks. She didn't think she'd ever seen her blush before. "My flawed instincts would have me believe that Levi is interested in me. I know it's utterly ridiculous. If I ever begin to trust my instincts, I come back to that benchmark; they tell me that Levi has an interest in me. This isn't the first time that notion has occurred either. So, now, do you understand?"

Autumn thought about it for a moment. "Hmm. I can see how, at face value, you might believe that was a flawed assumption, but I'm not so sure. You're not his usual type, but you are an attractive woman. I might have to do some observing of my own."

Paige waved a hand at her. "There's no need. Anyway. I'm going to leave instead."

"Oh. I thought you were going to come and have a drink?"

"So did I, but it seems that I just stepped a little farther outside my comfort zone than I can stand for now." Paige got to her feet. "Thank you for this. I appreciate it."

Autumn smiled. "Anytime. Maybe we should make it a weekly thing. Then you can schedule it in and make a commitment."

Paige smiled back at her. "You're rather perceptive yourself. I'll see you in the office tomorrow."

Autumn smiled to herself as she watched Paige leave, hoping that she'd keep up with this stepping out of her comfort zone.

She got to her feet and looked over to where the others were now all chatting and laughing. The blonde was leaning in talking to Matt, her hand resting on the back of his chair. Autumn frowned. Was Paige wrong about where his interest really lay? She strode over to join them. She was about to find out.

Chapter Eleven

The farther Matt edged away from Elle, the closer she leaned. He didn't dare look over at Autumn and Paige. He knew too well what Autumn would think if she saw this. She made no secret of the fact that she thought he still made the most of all the female attention he received. He didn't—because of her. Not because he wanted to impress her, but because she was the only one he was interested in. Elle was beautiful; anyone with eyes in their head could see that. But to Matt, it was like looking at a painting. He appreciated the visual, but there was no stirring in his blood—or his pants.

"Are you going to introduce me?"

Matt's shoulders sank. Maybe he should have paid attention to what Autumn was doing. Now she was standing behind him. And, judging by her tone, she wasn't impressed.

Levi grinned at her as Matt turned.

"Of course. These two lovely ladies are Elle and Tasha. I'm hoping that you'll get to hear them sing here in a little while. Ladies, please bow in the presence of our illustrious leader, the one and only, the legendary, Autumn Breese."

Matt had to hand it to Levi. He sucked up to Autumn like no other. But he did it in such a joking way that she never took offense.

The two girls didn't seem to think he was joking. They looked more awestruck in Autumn's presence than they had been by the guys.

Tasha was the first to step forward. She held out her hand, and Autumn shook it.

"Oh, my gosh! You have no idea what an honor it is to meet you, Miss Breese."

"Call me Autumn."

"Oh, okay. Autumn. I think you're amazing! You've done such a great job with McAdam Records. I mean, Clay's amazing. He's a legend. But before you came in … When that Ashley Devlin was in charge. I was worried. Then you came in and turned everything around, and now you have all the best artists in country music. You've made them successful commercially while letting them do their own thing artistically." Tasha stopped and looked around at them in embarrassment. "Sorry. I know I'm gushing here. But you have to understand. I'm meeting my idol."

Autumn smiled warmly at her. "Don't apologize. It's nice to be appreciated. Most people just see me as the bitch who keeps everyone in line."

Matt narrowed his eyes at her, but she didn't react.

"You know that's not true," said Levi. "We all adore you. And if anyone thinks you're a bitch, it's because you're a Babe In Total Control of Herself."

Matt scrunched his eyes up while he waited for her reaction to that.

To his relief, she laughed. "That's right. I am."

Elle extended her hand next. "I'm Elle. It truly is an honor to meet you."

Autumn shook with her and nodded. "Nice to meet you." She turned to Levi. "And what were you saying about hearing them sing?"

Levi raised an eyebrow at Matt.

"Levi suggested bringing in some female vocals for a couple of the remaining tracks. Jan and Alexa are out of town. So …"

Autumn nodded. "Are you playing here tonight?" she asked the girls.

Elle shook her head. "We've only been in town for a couple of days. We haven't lined up any real gigs yet. Last night we sang during the open mic session. That's how Levi heard us."

Matt wanted to kick Levi's ass. He'd assumed that they were here to hear the girls play.

Laurie saved him as she leaned on the bar. "Did I hear someone needs to jam?"

Matt smiled at her. "Kind of."

She gestured toward the stage with her arm. "Have at it. Charlie and Jax are on tonight, but they won't even be here to set up till seven. The stage and the sound system are all yours till then."

Matt raised an eyebrow at the girls. This was putting them on the spot.

Elle smiled confidently. "Awesome."

Tasha looked a little unsure of herself but followed her friend over to the stage. Levi bounded after them and West scrambled to follow.

Autumn blew out a sigh and looked at Lance. "Are you on board with this?"

"Can I reserve judgment till we hear them?"

Autumn laughed. "You mean you know as much about it as I do?"

"To be fair, I know a little more. We added some harmonies of our own this afternoon, and it sounded great. Then Levi suggested female harmonies and told us about the girls. He claims that they're awesome. But, as I said, I'd like to reserve judgment for now."

Autumn finally looked at Matt. A shiver ran down his spine as he held her gaze. Did she feel it, too? He hoped so. The way her eyes widened a little made him guess that maybe she did. "How do you feel about them?"

It felt like a loaded question. But maybe that was only because he felt guilty about acknowledging—even if only to himself—how hot Elle was. "Same as Lance. I think the idea has some merit, but we'll have to see if the reality lives up to it. Plus," he jerked his head toward the stage, "we'd have to see how the dynamics work out."

Autumn glanced over and nodded. "I guess we will."

"I can't believe that Levi isn't all over Elle." Bianca named the elephant in the room. "I'm a woman, and she's even making me stare." She smiled at Matt. "I'm sure you wouldn't mind having her around. She could make the album tour a lot more enjoyable for you. I could get some great coverage out of you and her dating."

Matt scowled at her. That was exactly the kind of thing he didn't want Autumn thinking about, let alone hearing. "I don't think so. The idea was only to bring them in on a couple of tracks, and that's only if they sound great. There wouldn't be any reason to bring them on tour."

Autumn shot him a glance. "Let's see how they sound first before we go making any decisions. It could be a great move for you."

He wanted to take her by the hand and lead her outside where he could talk to her honestly. He wanted to tell her that he didn't want Elle and Tasha or any other women coming out on the tour with them. He sure as hell didn't want her latching onto the idea that being seen out with Elle could be great PR for him. Of course, he couldn't say any of that with the others sitting there listening. All he could do was shrug. He couldn't argue, but he wasn't going to agree.

When the guys had helped them set up, Elle tapped on the microphone, and they all looked over.

She smiled at them. "Are you ready?"

"Sure, go ahead," called Autumn.

Matt pursed his lips as they started to sing an old song by The Corrs. Elle sang the intro in clear, crisp falsetto and then Tasha joined her, harmonizing beautifully. He sighed. He'd half hoped they wouldn't be any good.

Autumn sat down in West's seat and muttered, "Damn!"

"Couldn't have put it better myself," said Lance. "I hate it when Levi's right, but boy, was he right this time."

"What do you think, Matt?" asked Bianca.

He nodded. He could hardly pretend that they weren't amazing. "Yeah."

Autumn shot a look at him. "I'll bet taking them out on tour sounds a lot more appealing now."

He shook his head. "I don't think so."

"Are you crazy?" asked Lance. "Think of everything we could do with them."

He knew Lance meant musically, but the look on Autumn's face said she was thinking along different lines. Her lip curled slightly as she nodded. "You're right, Lance. And so were you, Bianca. This is a great development." She reached in her purse and pulled out her phone, tapping at the screen and staring for a few minutes. When she looked up again, she nodded briefly. "I need to get going."

That seemed strange to Matt. He'd thought she was checking something. He hadn't heard her phone go off with an incoming message.

She slung her purse over her shoulder.

"Do you need a ride?" asked Bianca.

"No. You stay. I'll call a ride share." She smiled around at them, not meeting Matt's gaze. "Tell the girls I think they're great. I'll see you all tomorrow." With that, she turned on her heel and left.

"Did I totally miss something?" asked Lance.

"I think we all did, but I have no idea what," said Bianca.

Matt blew out a sigh. He thought he had an idea what it was. He'd guess that while Autumn might still have been considering getting together with him, she'd just seen an opportunity that she believed would better serve his career—portraying him as being in a couple with Elle. The press would love that. It would guarantee a lot of coverage for the album and the tour. And that was more important to Autumn.

He downed the rest of his beer in one frustrated swig. "I'm out of here, too. I'm trusting you to set something up with the girls, Lance, and to keep those two in line."

Lance nodded. "I'll do my best."

"I can help," said Bianca. "But where are you going in such a hurry? Shouldn't you stick around?"

"Nah." Matt had heard all he needed to know that Elle and Tasha could make a worthy contribution to the remaining songs. He had no desire to talk to them about it. Lance could handle that. He did, on the other hand, have a very strong desire to talk to Autumn. She couldn't just palm him off on another woman like that. If she was too afraid to act on what she felt—and she couldn't deny after Seattle that she felt something—it didn't give her the right to dictate what direction his love life should take.

Laurie came back over just as he was getting down from his seat. "Where's Autumn?"

"She left," said Matt.

Laurie gave him an appraising look. "She didn't like the girls?"

Matt made a face at her. Laurie was something of a mom figure to him and to the other guys. She knew how he felt about Autumn. And even though he hadn't told her anything about Seattle, she seemed to know there was something going on. "She thinks they're great," he replied.

She blew out a sigh as she nodded. "Are you leaving, too?"

"Yup."

"Good luck."

"Thanks." How she knew he was going after Autumn and would probably need all the luck he could get, he had no clue. If the others weren't there, he might have asked for her advice. Instead, he made for the door.

"What does he need luck with?" he heard Bianca ask as he walked away.

~ ~ ~

Autumn paced up and down the sidewalk in front of the parking lot. She'd called a ride share, but it was taking its time. She almost wished she hadn't walked out of the tavern. She felt stupid. She'd felt an inexplicable surge of jealousy at the thought of Matt with Elle. She needed to get a grip. Elle was just the kind of girl who could be a great help to his career. That was what she was supposed to care about—his career. She was a professional. A professional whose job it was to do whatever was best to promote her artists. Elle could be a great promotional opportunity. And she was obviously interested in Matt.

She blew out a short sigh. She prided herself on being rational and businesslike. Yet, here she was reacting like some jealous girl. It wasn't like her. She didn't like feeling this way.

"Do you want a ride?"

She closed her eyes at the sound of his voice. Dammit. She didn't want to talk to him. She didn't want to hear what he thought about Elle and Tasha. She certainly didn't want to explain why she'd left the way she did. She turned around slowly. The sight of him took her breath away, just as it always did. He made her wish—if only for a moment—that she wasn't his label head. She'd rather be just a regular woman who could throw herself at him, succumb to his good looks and to the magnetic pull he had on her.

He stuffed his hands in his pockets and cocked his head to one side. "Would I be totally off if I thought you didn't really have to leave—you just wanted to?"

"No. I ..." Her denial was automatic. But the way he was looking at her from under his eyebrows stopped her in her tracks. He was being real with her—even if he was trying to be cute about it. She owed him the same.

She folded her arms across her chest and sighed. "No. You wouldn't."

He came a few steps closer. "Why?"

She shrugged. "It struck me that you all might bond better with the girls if I wasn't around."

He toed the ground with the tip of his cowboy boot and nodded. "I think they'll all bond better if I'm not there either. So, do you want a ride?"

"I have one coming."

"Mind if I share it?"

She pursed her lips. "Don't you have your truck?"

He shook his head, his eyes twinkling with amusement.

"So why did you offer me a ride?"

"I didn't mean in my truck."

She had to laugh.

He raised his shoulders. "You don't expect me to give up now, do you? You said you'd think about it. I've been waiting patiently. I respected your wishes and didn't harass you …"

She held his gaze for a long moment. She wanted to tell him that Elle would be better for his career. But she couldn't do it.

"Come on, baby girl. I've missed you. I've seen you less this week than I ever do. Just when I thought we were getting closer."

The car pulled up at the curb, and her phone beeped to let her know it had arrived. "Where are you going?" she asked as she opened the back door.

"I thought we could go grab a burger?" She stared at him for a long moment, and he grinned. "Go on. I know you want to. You haven't eaten yet. You love a big fat juicy burger, but you only get to eat them with me."

It was true, but she raised an eyebrow at him, wondering how he knew that.

He slid into the back seat and scooted over. When she got in after him, he grinned at her. "You're too much of a lady to go to a greasy burger joint by yourself. It's okay when you can blame it on me."

She laughed. He was right.

He slung his arm around her shoulders as the car pulled away. "If you think about it, I help you out in lots of little ways like that." He looked down into her eyes. "And if you wanted me to, I could come up with a few more."

All the little hairs on the back of her neck stood up and sent shivers chasing each other down her spine. There were less than six inches between his lips and hers. He narrowed the gap to maybe three, holding her gaze the whole way.

She wanted to resist, knew she should push him away, push him toward Elle, or someone else, but she couldn't damned well help it. She cupped her hand around the back of his head and drew him closer. If they were going to do this, then she couldn't put it all on him.

He brushed his lips over hers. It was the briefest touch, but it ignited something inside her. She leaned into him and kissed him deeply. His arms closed around her and he took over, his tongue exploring her, claiming her. She wanted to claim him right back. All thoughts of pairing him off with that blonde chick were gone. He was hers. *If only for tonight.* She hated the thought and pushed it away as soon as it came. She wanted him to be hers—she wanted to be his. Maybe that was unprofessional, unrealistic. She couldn't focus on thoughts. All she could focus on was the way his kisses made her feel. If she had to think about what it meant, all she could focus on was how they could make each other feel for the next few hours.

The car pulled up in front of her building in what felt like no more than a few minutes. Matt's lips only left hers when the car came to a halt. Autumn got out hurriedly, and Matt scrambled after her.

He dug in his pocket. "I can get it."

"It's all paid."

He looked puzzled. "Did those kisses steal your senses? You didn't pay, baby girl."

She laughed as the car pulled away. "I paid it on my phone. Have you never used a ride share before?"

"Nope. I drive or I walk."

Autumn shook her head. "I hate that you still walk around this town. You shouldn't, you know."

He put a finger to her lips. "Shh."

She narrowed her eyes at him. No one told her to shh!

He chuckled. "I know I'm dicing with death doing that, but that's not the way I want you to care about me."

Her heart beat faster.

"I want you to care about me like you started to in Seattle, like you showed me you do with your kisses just now. Do you want to?"

"What about the burger?"

He laughed and looked up at her building. "Now that we're here, maybe we should work up an appetite first and worry about food later."

"Maybe we should." Maybe she should have had the good sense to use her mouth to tell the driver to take them to his greasy burger joint instead of using it to kiss Matt the whole way. Now they were here—her apartment.

She looked at Matt, and he gave her a wry smile. "I'll leave if
you want me to, or we can go get that burger and then say
goodnight. You're the one calling the shots here. We can play
this any way you want to."

She nodded and walked toward the entrance. When he didn't
follow, she looked back.

"Am I coming?" he looked uncertain.

She chuckled. "I think it's safe to say that you will be."

Chapter Twelve

When Autumn let them into her apartment, she went straight to the fridge. "I'm guessing we could both use a beer?"

He smiled. "Please." This was as close to nervous as he'd ever seen her. He could understand it; he felt the same way. But it surprised him a little. It gave him hope. If she was nervous, it must matter to her. She didn't get nervous about negotiating or signing multi-million-dollar contracts, so maybe this mattered a lot?

She brought him a bottle and gestured for him to sit. He waited for her to sit first and then perched on the sofa beside her.

"Do you think we need to talk first?" she asked.

He laughed and raised his bottle to her. "First? Do you want to elaborate on what comes second?"

She made a face at him, and he was pleased to see her cheeks redden. "You know full well what I mean. Don't make this any harder, or I might kick you out and forget the whole thing."

He put a hand on her knee. He'd meant it to be an encouraging, supportive gesture, but it had a different effect—on both of them; he felt the lust stir in his pants, and he'd guess she felt the same way judging by the way her cheeks turned a darker shade of pink and her breasts heaved as she sucked in a deep breath. "I'm sorry. I can't help it. You're right. We should talk. Do you want to tell me what you're thinking?"

"Not really, but I will."

"Do you want to go first? Or will it be easier if you know what I'm thinking first?"

"I might as well spit it all out."

"Fire away, then, but just so you know—so you don't have any doubt. I want this. I want you. And I mean not just in the physical sense. I want there to be an us. I'm serious. I meant everything I said in Seattle."

She held his gaze for a long moment. "I want you. I want to do this—but I do mean in the physical sense. It's been building between us for years."

Matt's heart sank. Was she saying she just wanted to sleep with him—a one and done? "Is that all you want?" he couldn't help but ask.

"It should be. It has to be. How could anything else work? How could there be an us?"

He shrugged. "Same way every other couple manages it if you ask me. You get together. You spend your free time together. You have lots of fun, lots of sex. Annoy the hell out of each other, learn to accept and live with the not so perfect bits …"

"I don't mean that. I mean because of work."

"What does it matter?"

"It's not … it isn't right. There'd be a conflict of interests."

Matt laughed. "You really think so? I think my interests would still be aligned with the label's. I want to do my best for Clay and for you. Where would your conflict come from?"

Autumn shrugged. "I don't know. It feels wrong somehow—unprofessional."

"I don't see why. It's not like we work in a regular office, is it? I don't think anyone else would see it that way. We both know Clay wouldn't have a problem with it."

"I know."

He slid his hand a little farther up her leg. "We don't need to figure it all out right here and now. I just wanted to know where you stand—and make it very clear what I want out of this."

"Thanks."

"Back at Laurie's, I thought you were going to go hard on trying to set me up with Elle."

"I was."

"But you didn't. Why not?"

A small smile spread across her lips. "I'm not sure I want to tell you."

He smiled back, sensing a change in her mood. "Tell me," he breathed as he leaned closer.

She shook her head.

It didn't matter anyway. He didn't want to hear or think about Elle. He wanted to get closer to Autumn. He slid his arm around her waist and drew her closer. "Have we talked enough?"

She nodded and slid her arms up around his shoulders. "Way too much."

He smiled and lowered his mouth to hers. Her lips were so full and soft, her kisses tasted so sweet. Before he knew how they got there, they were lying on the sofa limbs tangled, tongues dueling. She moaned into his mouth as he pressed his cock between her legs. Unlike her jeans which had kept him at bay last time they'd been in this position, the skirt she wore was rucked up around her waist. The lacy panties she wore underneath made him even harder. He tried not to think about her underwear whenever they were at work, but now he knew this was what she wore, he wasn't sure he'd be able to think about anything else.

He leaned his head back to look into her eyes and cupped her cheek in his hand. "You're making my dreams come true here."

She chuckled. "I probably shouldn't admit this, but me, too."

He gave her a stern look. "You've dreamed about this?"

She cocked one shoulder. "I think fantasized might be a more honest description."

He pinned her down with his weight and slid his hand between her legs. "You meant to tell me that you've thought about what it would be like if I did this?"

He slipped his fingers inside her panties, and his cock throbbed at the little sound she made and the way she bit her bottom lip as she nodded.

"I think about it all the time," he breathed as he began to stroke her. "I think about how you'll feel, how you'll taste …" Her eyes widened at that, and he teased her open with his fingertips. "I never dreamed you'd be this hot and this wet for me." He slowly dipped his finger inside her. "Or this tight."

She nodded and rocked her hips slightly. The movement made them both tense. "I want you, Matt. Not just your finger."

He withdrew his hand and kneeled back to look down at her. "We're not at work now, baby girl. You don't get to call all the shots here. You'll get what you want, but you'll get it when I say."

She frowned, but he stroked her again, this time, tormenting her clit through her panties. When she was moaning again, he hooked his fingers inside her panties and pulled them down. "You'll get me and my fingers and my tongue, but not in that order."

He stroked the insides of her thighs and loved the way she writhed under his touch. He dipped his head and nibbled her thigh, making her fingers come down and tangle tightly in his hair. "Oh, God, Matt, yes!"

He worked her with his tongue and his fingers, just as promised, loving the way she moved so eagerly, so willingly with him. When he felt her tense, he took her clit between his lips and sucked as he thrust his fingers deep and hard over and over until she came for him. Her inner muscles gripped him hard. He came close himself. It was such a turn on that she'd give herself up for him so openly.

"Matt, oh, Matt," she gasped over and over until her orgasm subsided, and she finally lay still.

He crawled up beside her and wrapped her in his arms, wanting her to feel close to him. "Was it like that when you thought about it?"

She shook her head and gave a small chuckle. "No. It was nowhere near as good as that. You're a talented man, Mr. McConnell."

"I aim to please."

"Well, your aim was perfect. I think I should return the favor."

He sucked in a deep breath. "Do you mean what I think you mean?"

She gave him a sly smile. Her fingers had already found his zipper and were starting to help him out of his jeans. "I sure do."

He shook his head and moved his hips away. "Next time?"

She gave him a puzzled frown. "You don't want me to?"

He gave a half strangled sounding groan. "Oh, I want you to. But I might like it a little too much—and a little too soon, if you get my drift? How about we say next time? In fact, if you're calling it returning the favor—then you'll kind of owe me one, and that can be my guarantee that we get to do this again."

She held his gaze for a long moment. "You're serious about this not being a one and done, aren't you?"

He stroked her cheek. "Evidently, I'm much more serious than you realize, baby girl."

~ ~ ~

"I don't know how it could work, Matt." Autumn looked up into his eyes. She was feeling all warm and glowy after the orgasm he'd just given her. Her brain felt fuzzy, and her body melted against him. Lust still hummed in her veins. She should feel satisfied, but he'd only woken her desires; she wanted more of him. But somehow the conversation had taken this turn to something bigger.

The look on his face, the way his palm cupped her cheek, everything about him told her that he was deadly serious about this. The warm and fuzzy part of her wanted to just roll with it. The voice of caution in the back of her head was telling her to stop it now. Her doubts about whether he was genuine had all shriveled and died over the course of the last couple of hours. Now she was more concerned about whether they should start something they couldn't see through.

"I told you. It'll work however we want it to." He cocked his head to one side. "I guess the big question is, do you want it to?"

She held his gaze for a long moment. She did, but she wasn't sure she wanted to commit to saying so. Instead, her fingers returned to their work, getting him out of his pants. He resisted for a moment, but she pressed her lips into his neck. He smelled so good. She nibbled her way up to his ear, and he groaned and gave in, helping her to get rid of his jeans and his boxers.

She watched him pull his shirt up over his head and off. She'd seen his naked chest enough times, but it still sent shivers racing through her. This time it was just for her.

As if reading her mind, he smiled and said, "You've seen it all before. I, on the other hand ..." He eyed her breasts and ran his tongue over his bottom lip before biting down on it.

She smiled as she unbuttoned her blouse. He loved her breasts. She already knew that. She caught him looking at them often enough in meetings. His eyes darkened with lust as she took off the blouse, glad that she'd worn her favorite lacy bra and panty set today. She hadn't had time for guys or dating for a long time. But when she'd found herself slipping into the habit of wearing plain white cotton underwear a couple of months ago, she'd gone out and splurged on lacies that were sexy and comfortable at the same time.

Matt reached out and closed his hands around her breasts. Her nipples stiffened under his touch and sent sparks flying through her, reigniting the heat between her legs.

Matt closed his eyes as he touched her through the lace. "Do you know how many times I've fantasized about doing this?" he asked in a low voice.

She smiled. "Probably not as many as I have." She reached around her back and unhooked the bra. In her version of the fantasy, he'd always been touching her naked skin, and she couldn't wait any longer.

He lowered his head and flicked each nipple in turn with his tongue, making her moan.

"I could worship these babies for hours," he breathed.

She laughed. "Maybe next time. They're very pleased to finally meet you. But there's another introduction I've been needing you to make." She closed her fingers around him and pushed him back, so he was lying against the cushions.

He looked down and watched as she stroked the length of him. "You want to meet that guy?"

She nodded.

"He's very, very glad to meet you."

Autumn dipped her head and swirled her tongue over the tip of him. He tensed and brushed her hair away from her face. "Next time?" He looked pained.

She bobbed her head and closed her lips around him, making him groan.

"Please, baby girl?" He put his hands on her hips. "I told you I wanted to give you a ride tonight."

Autumn gave him one last flick of her tongue and then straddled him. "I'm hardly going to turn that down, am I?"

"I hoped not." He started to stroke her, but she shook her head. She didn't need any more encouragement than the feel of his hot hard cock, throbbing between her legs, pushing at her entrance. She grasped him tight, eliciting another moan as she guided him inside.

"Jesus, Autumn!" He sounded desperate as she lowered herself slowly onto him. "Fuck me, don't torment me."

She chuckled. "Patience, lover. We're getting there."

He gave her a wry smile. "I might get there, too, before you at this rate."

"Don't worry, I'll be right there with you." She was on the verge now. She'd needed to go slowly. It'd been a long time for her, and he was a handful, to say the least. She was the one in torment as his thick hard shaft stretched her and filled her. The way he pulsated inside her might send her over the edge at any moment.

He closed his hands around her hips and thrust, driving home and making her scream. Her breasts bounced as he thrust wildly, and she rode him hard, taking him deeper and deeper. He held her gaze the whole time, the connection between their eyes just as intimate if not more so than the one between their bodies. The frantic coupling as they moved together, taking each other higher and higher until Autumn felt like she was about to fly away. He gasped and tensed and then found his release, taking her with him as his orgasm triggered hers. He was the only solid point in a universe that melted around her as waves of pleasure crashed through her.

When the waves finally receded, she slumped down onto his chest, and he closed his arms around her, tangling his fingers in her hair.

"Damn, baby girl," he breathed.

"Double damn," she murmured.

"Finally."

"Yup, finally."

He chuckled against her neck, sending aftershocks through her. She shuddered and rolled off him. He wrapped her up in his arms. "It's hard to believe that you've wanted this as long as I have."

She looked into his eyes. "Probably longer. But I couldn't let it show. Couldn't let you know."

"Why, though? We could have been together all this time. Doing this …" he ran his hand down her back, making her quiver again "… every night."

"No. We couldn't. I'm not even sure that we should now."

His arm tightened around her. "Don't say that."

"I'm not saying I don't want to. Just that I'm not sure that it's the best idea."

"It is. It's the best idea ever. Don't go backing out on me now, will you?"

"No." She didn't think she'd be able to even if she thought she should. Something had shifted between them last weekend in Seattle. Tonight, they'd cemented the change in their relationship. She felt it. Somewhere deep inside her—maybe it was in her heart, even if some people claimed she didn't have one—she felt that this was a major turning point in their lives. She just had to hope that it was a turn for the better.

Chapter Thirteen

When Matt opened his eyes the next morning, he immediately turned his head to check. It was real! Autumn was there. He was here. In her bed. After a great night. Not just a great night, but the best night of his life so far. She was amazing; they were amazing together. They'd made love a second time. Then he'd called out for dinner. The burgers weren't as good as they would have been if they'd gone to his favorite burger joint, but he'd swear they tasted even better given that he got to eat one sitting on Autumn's sofa with her wearing just his shirt. Maybe it was just that they were both starving after their exertions. She was quite something. She was as bold in bed as she was in every other aspect of her life. He loved that about her. He smiled to himself. Love was a strong word, but he was pretty sure that love was what he felt for the strong, beautiful woman who lay beside him.

She opened her eyes a few moments later, and his heart leaped in his chest. He was anxious to see how she'd react this morning. He was prepared for her to try to brush him off. He knew how she felt about her work. It was the most important thing in the world to her. She based her identity on her career.

And there was the not-so-small matter of her love for and loyalty to Clay. Clay had been like a father to her and her sister. She ran the label for him, and in a way, Matt could see that running it well was the best way she knew to show him how much she loved him. However important her career was to her, Matt understood. But he didn't see how getting involved with him could take away from it in any way. Jeez, if she ended up marrying him, that would solidify his relationship with McAdam Records in the most concrete way.

He relaxed when she smiled slowly at him. "Good morning."

He slid his arm around her waist and drew her to him. "Good morning. Did you sleep well?"

"I did—you'd think I was exhausted or something. You wore me out."

He smiled. "I think it was mutual. We're going to need to build up our stamina. I don't know about you, but it's been a long time for me. What do you say, should we do it again tonight to get me back in practice?"

She laughed. "If practice makes perfect, then you don't need any practice."

He enjoyed the compliment, but he'd asked to test her reaction. Would she want to see him again tonight—or was she going to revert to her insistence that this had to be a one and done. He wasn't going to accept it if she did. He'd chipped away at her resistance all these years; he wasn't about to give up now. He just needed to know what he was dealing with.

"Sweet-talker," he said with a grin. "You'd never say that about my singing or guitar playing. Even the best need to practice regularly, right?"

She nodded. "That's true. So, then, I guess, in the interests of helping you maintain your expertise, yeah, why not? Let's do it again tonight."

Matt's heart raced. "Awesome. We can go for dinner when you get done in the office, then we can come back here or go to my place if you prefer."

Her smile had faded. "How about I meet you here at say, ten o'clock?"

"Do you have other plans?"

She lifted a shoulder. "I have plenty of work to do. I just think it's best if we keep what we're doing here to ourselves."

Matt frowned and dropped a kiss on her lips. "Are you ashamed of me?"

She chuckled. "No. It's not my reputation I'm worried about. It's yours."

"How could being with you hurt my reputation? It'd probably help. It'd no doubt get a lot of the coverage you're always trying to get me. It'd be a big story."

She shook her head. "No. The fans like to think of you as single—available, so they can believe that one day they might meet you and be the one you fall for."

He pursed his lips. "Hypocrite."

She scowled. "I am not!"

"Yes, you are!" he said with a short laugh. "At the bar last night, you were trying to palm me off on Elle—saying that would be good press for me. Make your mind up. Is being in a relationship good PR or bad?"

She chewed on her bottom lip and at least had the good grace to look contrite. "It's not that simple. I'm not being hypocritical. The circumstances are different."

"How?"

She shrugged. "Fans love a celebrity couple. It's not so interesting when a celebrity is dating someone from the back office."

He shook his head at her. "We should just drop this subject now before I get mad at you. For one thing, Elle isn't a celebrity. She's a wannabe backup signer. You, on the other hand, are not just someone from the back office. Come off it, Autumn. You know that. You're one of the most powerful women in this town. And unlike most of the execs in town, you're not just a name to the fans either—you're face, a very beautiful face." He dropped a kiss on her lips. "That guy in the restaurant in Seattle—Eddie whatever his name was. He proved my point. So, you're only arguing yourself into a corner. If you want to keep the fact that we're seeing each other under wraps for a little while till you get your head around it, that's fine. I can respect that. But I can't respect the bullshit excuses you're feeding me."

She gave him a rueful smile. "I taught you well, grasshopper."

"What do you mean?"

"When we first started working together, you were too polite to call anyone out on their bullshit. Now, you're almost as good at it as I am."

He smiled, relieved that she wasn't mad at him for calling her out. "I had a great teacher. The best." He nuzzled his face into her neck, hoping that she'd be interested in starting the day with a bang.

She cupped his face between her hands and brought him up to look her in the eye. "We don't have time for that. I need to get to the office, and you have studio time booked."

He planted a kiss on her lips. "I can make it quick."

She rolled her eyes. "Not a great way to persuade me, McConnell."

He had to laugh. "Another lesson in straight-shooting; thanks, baby girl. I think my enthusiasm just waned anyway. Want me to make you some coffee while you take a shower?"

She wrapped her arms around him and pressed herself against him, reigniting his enthusiasm instantly. "Now, *that* is the way to do it. You know coffee is the way to my heart." She planted a kiss on his lips and then rolled over and climbed out of bed.

He watched her naked ass sway as she went into the bathroom, then he rolled out of bed himself. Tempting as it was to follow her into the shower, he knew he'd earn more brownie points by making coffee. And even if she didn't want people to know about them just yet, she had agreed to spend the night with him again tonight, so he wouldn't have to suffer through his need for her for much more than twelve hours. Which was nothing after all the years he'd already waited.

Autumn was busy all day. She didn't have time to sit around mooning over Matt, even if she wanted to. To be fair, she did want to. She just didn't want to admit that to herself. Could it really be as simple as he thought? After all this time of avoiding his advances—by dismissing them as nothing more than egotistical flirting, and therefore claiming that she wasn't interested—could she now just turn around, do a total one-eighty, and walk straight into a relationship with him? Probably. Now that she'd finally admitted her attraction to the guy, her irritation with him had evaporated—mostly. She knew she'd have to give it some time to see if she found him as infuriating again once this initial infatuation wore off.

Even if she could get over her own resistance so quickly, would it be a good idea to let the rest of the world know what was going on between them? Probably not. She had a grace period; she knew that. Matt was happy to wait while she wrapped her head around the change in their relationship. But how long would he be willing to wait? How did she feel about telling Clay? She shuddered at the thought—and not in a good way. Clay thought the world of Matt, and he was a father figure to her. Over the years, he'd made no secret of the fact that he thought the two of them would be good together. But what if they weren't good? What if it ended horribly? Even if it ended awkwardly. It'd be bad for the label—and it would disappoint Clay. Then there was her sister. Summer was another one who'd believed that she and Matt would get together someday. She'd be ecstatic to be proved right. But Autumn didn't need that kind of pressure, not while she figured out how real it could be.

She looked up at the sound of a knock on her door. "Come in."

"Hey, Autumn. Sorry to bother you." Zack, one of the company pilots, came just inside the door. "I'll only keep you a minute. I came in to drop some forms off with HR. I wanted to see if you're free later. You promised Luke and me a raincheck on that dinner invite."

Autumn's mind raced. She had said that she and Matt would have dinner with them one night this week. She didn't want to back out, but she'd much rather have the evening with Matt.

Zack smiled. "No worries. I only stopped by on the off chance."

She blew out a sigh. "Yeah, sorry. It wouldn't work tonight, and you guys are heading back to Summer Lake for Clay tomorrow, right?"

"That's right. The way the plan stands at the moment, we won't be back here for a couple of weeks. We're taking Marianne and Laura to San Antonio next week."

"Oh, that's right. They're going to see Laura's Aunt Cindy. She told me about that."

"Yeah. We'll be there for a few days and then back at the lake waiting to hear Clay's plans. Unless you need us for anything in the meantime, of course."

She shook her head. "I don't have any travel in my schedule for a while. Not until Matt's tour starts, then I guess I'll have to pop out to check on him occasionally."

Zack chuckled. "He's not that bad, is he?"

Autumn couldn't hold back a smile. "He's pretty great, actually, but don't ever tell him I said that. I think on this tour it's going to be more of a case of keeping the others in line. There may be two new, hot backup singers traveling with them. You already know what Levi's like and the new guy, West, made a beeline for one of the girls yesterday. It could prove interesting."

Zack nodded. "I don't envy you. You're amazing at your job, but I don't know how you do it."

"Thanks. I enjoy it. Keeping horny musicians in line isn't my favorite part, but it goes with the territory. How are you enjoying your job?" She felt bad that she still hadn't made time to check in with him and Luke. They took care of all the travel arrangements and were as friendly and helpful as you could hope.

Zack's grin gave her his answer before he spoke. "I love it. I love that I get to fly—especially that Luke and I get to fly together. I love that I get to be home as much as I do in between flights."

"I'll bet Maria likes that aspect of the job, too." Zack was engaged to a wonderful girl. Autumn had met her a few times on her trips to Summer Lake to visit with Clay. She liked her a lot. The two of them had had a rough ride in the beginning from what Autumn understood. Some crazy had been stalking Zack, threatening to kill him. That was all over now, and the guy was behind bars.

"She does. I think she likes that I'm not there all the time. She's an independent soul. She has her girlfriends, she loves her job, and she likes to spend time by herself. So, it works out great. We appreciate the time we do get to spend together, and we're both busy doing things we enjoy when we're apart."

"That sounds like the ideal relationship."

Zack smiled. "I think so. You should try it."

She turned her frown into a smile just as fast as it appeared. Zack didn't know about her and Matt. Although thinking back on it now, maybe he had some idea. He and Luke had talked Matt up when they landed in Seattle, and they'd flat out refused to join the two of them for dinner. She narrowed her eyes at Zack, wondering if he'd give away how much he knew.

He didn't. He just shrugged. "I mean, I know you're a busy lady. If you were to start seeing someone ... I ..." He smiled. "I think I'm going to shut up and go now."

She smiled back. "Okay. It was good to see you. Thanks for stopping in. Let me know when you and Luke are going to be back, and we'll set something up."

"Okay. Sounds good. We will."

After he'd gone, she looked up at the clock on the wall. Four o'clock. Six more hours until Matt would show up at her place. She wished she'd said earlier. When she'd suggested that time, she'd still been thinking that maybe she could pretend that this was just about sex. They weren't making a date to go out and enjoy each other's company; they were simply setting a time when he could come over to enjoy each other's body. That was bullshit, though. She hadn't even managed to fool herself. Maybe she should text him to see if he wanted to come earlier. She could order in some Chinese food or something.

She drummed her fingers on the desk. She could text him, or she could stop by the studio and see how things were going. She wasn't sure that was such a good idea. Especially since she was the one who wanted to keep what was going on between them a secret, but she did want to see him. She nodded and got to her feet. She hadn't been near the studio this week because of what happened in Seattle. She would normally have been down there most days. It was time to get back to normal—or perhaps to figure out what the new normal was going to be.

When she got there and peered through the glass in the door, she could see straight through into the booth—and wished she hadn't come. Matt was standing at the mic and Elle was standing way too close beside him, her shoulder touching his as they sang.

Autumn made a face and turned away. She didn't need to see that. She pursed her lips and stood there for a moment. Part of her wanted to go back up to her office and forget she had seen it. But that part of her wasn't going to win. She pushed the door open and went in. She wasn't the jealous kind. She might be feeling a little rattled right now, but she had a feeling most women would, seeing their man standing with Elle like that. But jealousy was a product of insecurity, and Autumn wasn't insecure.

She didn't need to react in any way. Matt wasn't doing anything wrong. Neither was Elle, for that matter. She was doing exactly what she'd been brought in to do, which was to sing harmonies. Matt was gorgeous—in personality as well as in looks. Autumn couldn't blame Elle for making a play for him. She smiled to herself. She might unfairly dislike her a little bit for it, but she couldn't blame her!

"Hey." Lance looked up from his seat at the board. "What do you think? Don't they sound great together?"

"They do. How's it working out?"

"Like a dream," said Lance with a grin. "We're going to be finished ahead of schedule at this rate. The girls are so easy to work with. They're eager to learn, eager to please. I only need to tell them once what I want, and they get it."

"That's great. Where's everyone else?"

Lance looked a little guilty. "Tasha already had an appointment this afternoon, so we got all her stuff down early. Levi and West got done, too."

"So, it's just you, Matt, and Elle left?"

"Yeah. Matt didn't mind waiting since everyone else had other stuff to get to."

Autumn glanced through the window. "And I'm sure Elle volunteered to stay till the end with him, right?"

"That's right. I get the impression that she'd be more than happy to pair up with Matt, if that's what you want to push to help with PR."

"That's *so* not what I want!" Autumn snapped before she could stop herself.

Lance looked taken aback. "Sorry. I must have misunderstood. I thought yesterday ..."

She gave him an apologetic smile. "No, you're right. But that was yesterday. I had a change of heart."

"Okay."

She'd wondered if Lance would have any inkling of what she meant. Apparently not. She glanced at Matt and Elle again. They still hadn't noticed her. "I'll see you tomorrow, Lance."

He frowned. "You're leaving?"

"Yeah. I just wanted to check in."

Chapter Fourteen

Matt was pleased with the way the day had gone. Tasha and Elle were great. He loved their sound and adding them in would make the last few songs great. He'd thought he knew which song he wanted to feature as the single, but after today, he wasn't so sure. The track they'd laid down today was a strong contender, and he could see a couple of the others that they still had to record being options, too.

He went to stand in front of his windows. He loved this view of the city. He loved his apartment. He wanted to invite Autumn over here soon. She'd been here often enough, but things were different now. He turned back to look around. He'd done okay for himself, and the apartment reflected that. He smiled as a crazy thought struck him. If they got together for real, would she move in here with him? He'd go to her place if that was what she wanted—the way he felt he'd go live anywhere she wanted to. But he liked the idea of her moving in here.

He shook his head. He was getting way ahead of himself. Tonight, he was going over to her place. That was good enough for now. It was better than he'd expected. He'd had a text waiting from her when he came out of the booth. She'd suggested he should come earlier—not wait until ten if he didn't want. That made him happy. He'd been okay with waiting, but he liked the idea of getting to spend the whole evening with her much better.

He'd showered and gotten dressed—in three different outfits before finally settling on the jeans and black T-shirt he was wearing now. He picked up his wallet and his keys. She'd said he could come earlier, so he didn't see the point in wasting any time.

His phone beeped with a text just as he reached his truck in the parking garage. He pulled it out of his pocket, hoping it was her.

It wasn't. It was West.

You free tonight?

Matt frowned and texted back.

Nope. I have plans. You should try Levi if you want to hang out.

He opened the truck and got in, then waited a few moments to see if West replied.

I need to talk to you.

Shit. Why now? Matt wanted to blow him off, tell him they could talk tomorrow, but West already knew that.

Give me a few. I'll call you.

He started up the truck and waited until he was out on the street before he called.

"Hey." West's voice boomed through the speakers, reminding Matt that he'd had Willy Nelson blasting last time he drove. He lowered the volume as fast as he could.

"Hey. What's up?"

"Is this a bad time?"

"No, it's fine. I'm driving. I was just getting in the truck when you texted."

"Ah. Sorry. I can wait. You going anywhere fun?"

Matt opened his mouth to tell him he was going to Autumn's, but he stopped himself just in time. She didn't want anyone to know yet, and he had to respect that. Even though West had a good idea of what was going on anyway. "Just to see a friend."

West chuckled. "And by the way you're so obviously not saying it, I think I can guess who that friend is, right?"

"Probably. But if you don't say it, I won't have to say it either, and that way, I won't have told you."

"Fair enough. I'll leave that subject alone. Although it's kind of the subject I wanted to talk to you about."

Matt was silent as he came to a stop at a traffic light. "Go on," he said when it was evident West wasn't going to continue.

"I mean, the subject of getting involved with people we work with."

"Ah." Matt had a feeling he knew what West was getting at, and he wasn't talking about him and Autumn. "Tasha?" he asked.

"Yup."

"It could get awkward."

"I know. That's why I'm sitting here talking to you on the phone instead of out with her. It took me everything I had not to ask her out tonight."

"Do you think she's even interested?"

West chuckled. "I want to think so, but she seems, I dunno, kind of wary, complicated maybe."

"And you want to get involved with complicated?"

"Hell, no. I don't want to, but I don't know if I'm going to be able to stay away. I think I was half hoping that you'd give me a hard no. Make the decision for me and then I have to live with it."

Matt chuckled. "Sorry, bud. I'm not big on laying down rules. It's generally accepted with the guys that we don't get involved with people we work with—but I'm not going to be a hypocrite. I guess the best advice I can give you is, take some time. Think about it first. Get to know her better. You might find out that hers is the kind of complicated you don't want to go anywhere near."

West sighed. "I know. You're right. Has there been any more talk about them coming on tour?"

"Not as such, no. But after today's session, I have to admit that it might not be a bad idea. And if they do, you might regret any hasty decisions you make now."

"Yup. Thanks, Matt. I'll let you go. I think I'm just going to tell myself that you said no and live with that."

Matt felt bad for him. He knew how it felt to be interested in someone you worked with and not be able to do anything about it—until now. "Maybe you should get to know her as a friend? Hang out with her as much as you want to, but don't cross the line. That way, if there is going to be something between you, you'll already have a good foundation built by the time the tour's over. And, in the meantime, you'll get to know if she's someone you really want to be with. There's a lot to be said for taking it slowly."

"You're right. Thanks, Matt. I'll see you in the morning."

"Yeah, see ya. And if you're at a loose end tonight, take yourself to Laurie's. She's good people, and you'll no doubt run into people you know there. Levi will probably be there, maybe Corbin."

"I think I'll do that. You have yourself a good night."

"I will." Matt smiled to himself as he hung up. He planned to have a very good night.

~ ~ ~

Autumn hurried out of the bathroom and picked her phone up off the bed. She clutched her towel to her as she answered.

"This is Autumn."

"This is Matt."

She smiled. "Hey."

"Hey. Are you ready for some company, or am I too early?"

A shiver of anticipation ran down back, and she clutched her towel tighter. "I just got out of the shower. I—" She was about to say she'd be ready in less than fifteen minutes, but Matt cut her off.

"I'd better hurry up then, huh? What are you wearing right now?"

She chuckled. "Right now? Just a towel."

"Sounds perfect. I'm just pulling up."

"Okay. I'll get dressed."

"Do you have to?"

"You want me to greet you with a towel and a smile?"

"You could lose the towel."

She laughed. "I think I'll hang on to it."

"Not for long. I'm in the lobby."

"See you in a minute then." She ran back into the bathroom. She hadn't even dried her hair yet. She had no makeup on. So what? He knew what she looked like. If he wanted perfect, he'd do better to look elsewhere.

She ran a hand through her hair and shrugged at herself. She was good enough the way she was. If that wasn't good enough for Matt, then he could always go find Elle. She hurried to answer the door when he rang the bell.

"Damn!" He ran a hand through his hair as he let his gaze travel over her. "I thought you'd get dressed." He finally looked back up to meet her gaze. "That might be the best outfit I've ever seen you in."

She laughed. "Come on in. Don't just stand there in the hallway. I don't mind you seeing, but I don't want the neighbors to."

He grinned and leaned in the doorway. "I think I'd be doing a public service if I paraded you around the building in that towel."

She made a face at him. "Don't push your luck, McConnell." She started to close the door on him. "If you're coming in, you'd better be quick."

He was quick. He stepped inside and closed the door behind him with his foot, closed his arms around her and backed her against the wall. She loved the feel of him pressed up against her and slid her arms up around his neck. "Hello."

"Hi." He dropped a peck on her lips and slid his hands under the towel to cup her ass. "I couldn't wait any longer. I haven't stopped thinking about you all day."

She smiled. "I couldn't stop thinking about you either."

He grinned. "You couldn't?"

"No. I tried to. I kept busy, distracted myself, but you, pain in my ass that you are, just wouldn't get out of my head."

"That makes me happy. Happy to know that you were thinking about me, and even happier that you don't mind telling me that you were. I didn't know how you were going to play this whole thing."

She met his gaze. "I didn't know how I wanted to play it—I'm still not entirely sure that it's a great idea. But there are a couple of things I do know."

"Yeah? Like what?"

"I know that I don't play games—you know that, too. And I also know that I value you and our friendship too much to not be up front with you—about the good and the bad."

He stroked a strand of damp hair off her forehead. It was such a small gesture, but it turned her insides to mush. It shifted something inside her. For the first time, she saw him as more than just the Matt she knew. He was still the loveable, irritating friend she'd known for years, but with that gesture, she felt like he could be her man. She held her breath as she looked up into his eyes.

He looked puzzled. "What? You just said you're going to be upfront with me, and then your expression changed, and you look like you have something to tell me—something I'm not going to like."

She shook her head and buried her face in his neck. She didn't have a problem with being direct, that was normal for her. What wasn't normal was admitting her feelings—even to herself—let alone talking about them.

He closed his hand around the back of her head and held her close. She could feel his heart hammering in his chest. "It's okay, baby girl. Whatever it is, you can tell me. I can take it."

"It's not a bad thing. It's a good thing." She felt him relax a little. "It just hit me that this could be something real; that's all."

"That's all?" He held her shoulders and leaned back to look at her face. "That's all? That's huge! I thought it'd take me months to get you to see that."

She laughed. "You're a cocky bastard, McConnell."

"Nope. That implies that I'm overly confident. I'm not. I'm just confident. I have been for years. You're going to be my woman. I'm going to be your man. I'm in it for the long haul, no matter how long it takes. I'm just glad that it might not take as long as I thought."

She gave him a stern look. "I'm not saying I'm going to rush into anything."

"I know. I don't need you to. I just need to know that we're on the same page; that you understand what I'm going for here and that you're open to it."

She almost asked him to clarify what he was going for—to spell out where he wanted this to go, but she thought better of it. She had an idea of what he was thinking, but that was too big an idea to entertain at this point, and there was no need to bring it up. Instead, she said, "I'm open to seeing where we can take this, but I'd still like to keep it quiet for a while."

He nodded grudgingly. "Okay, but not for too long. It's hard. I want to tell the whole world. I want to share how happy I am, and I want to let ..." He stopped without finishing.

She had a good idea of what he meant though. "You want to let other women know that you're not available, so you don't have to deal with their advances?"

"Yeah. I figured you'd tell me how cocky I am if I said that, though."

"That's not being cocky; it's just a part of your reality. Was Elle hitting on you today?"

He pursed his lips. "Did you see?"

She nodded gravely.

"Sorry. I know it couldn't have looked good."

She shrugged. "I didn't enjoy seeing the two of you in the booth together, but I get it. I know you. If you wanted to go after her, you wouldn't be going after me."

"Thank you."

"What for?"

"For knowing who I am, for trusting me. I have no interest in her, or in any other woman. You're the only one for me, Autumn Breese."

She looked up into his eyes. He was deadly serious. It took her breath away. This was all happening so fast. Just a week ago, he'd still been the same Matt he'd always been. Fun, infuriating if lovable; her friend, the bane of her life. Now he was holding her in his arms, telling her she was the one for him, and she was telling him that she trusted him and wanted to see where this could go. "I can't believe I'm saying this, but I believe you."

"Good. And you don't need to worry about Elle. She knows."

Autumn frowned. "What did you tell her?"

"Not about you. I just told her that I'm seeing someone, but we're keeping it secret."

"Shit. Now there are going to be all kinds of rumors spreading about who your mystery woman might be."

"She promised me she wouldn't tell a soul. Well, no one except Tasha. I thought it'd make life easier if they both know."

"I suppose. I can see the sense in that."

He smiled. "Thanks. See, when you're not perpetually pissed off at me, you can see that I'm not such an asshole, right?"

She laughed. "I never thought of you as an asshole. Even I know you're a good guy. But you are a pain in the ass."

He squeezed her cheeks, kneading her with his fingers. "This ass?"

She nodded and melted against him, loving the way his hard cock pressed into her belly. "Yeah. That ass."

"Do you think we should take it to bed, and I can massage it, try to make up for all the trouble I've caused it over the years?"

"Mm-hmm." She took hold of his hand and led him to the bedroom.

Chapter Fifteen

"So, what do you think, guys; are we going to rock this tour?"

Five smiling faces nodded eagerly back at him, and Matt grinned. The last couple of weeks had flown by. The album was finished. This had been the last rehearsal before they would take off on tour on Thursday. He was pumped. Bringing in Tasha and Elle had added a whole new element to their sound, and he knew that the fans would love it. He'd even written a couple of new songs that featured the girls' harmonies. They hadn't made it onto the album, but they'd test them out on tour. The girls were coming along. He hadn't liked the idea at first, but it made sense. There were no downsides to bringing them along. He cast a glance at West who was watching Tasha chat with Lance. At least, he hoped there wouldn't be any problems. Tasha was sweet and, so far, West seemed to be following his advice of getting to know her as a friend and not taking it any further than that.

"We're totally going to rock it," Levi said with a grin, "and this is it now, right? We're free until the bus leaves on Thursday morning?"

"That's right." Matt raised an eyebrow at him. "I take it that means you have plans and we shouldn't expect to see you until the bus pulls out?"

Levi swaggered his shoulders. "That'd be right. I have to do what I can for the ladies of Nashville before I leave. They're going to have to do without until we get back."

Lance rolled his eyes. "Don't you think you should be resting up before you take care of the ladies of Orlando, and then the ladies of Atlanta?"

Levi laughed. "Resting up? That's not how it works; I need to build up. First, I'll do my best to please the home crowd here, then I'll do my best to satisfy the ladies all around the country."

Elle shook her head. "You're joking, right?" She looked at Lance. "Please tell me he's joking?"

Lance shook his head. "Sorry. He's deadly serious."

Levi grinned at her. "Sorry, sweetheart, but since you're coming with us, you don't get any."

Elle gave him a disdainful look. "I wouldn't want any, thanks."

Levi laughed. "Only because you think you might get some elsewhere—but don't hold your breath on that either." He winked at Matt.

Matt was surprised to see Elle's cheeks flush deep red. "I don't think that at all," she snapped. "I'm not like you. I respect when someone is in a relationship. I know Matt has a girlfriend!"

Matt's heart sank as Levi, Lance, and West all swung their heads to look at him incredulously.

He shrugged and got to his feet. He knew he wouldn't be able to avoid their questions, but he didn't want to answer them in front of the girls. "I guess we're done here. I'll see you all Thursday."

He made his way to the door and managed to get through it before Levi and Lance caught up with him.

"What the hell is she talking about?" asked Levi.

Lance gave him a hard stare. "I had a feeling there was something going on with you, but why would you tell Elle and not us?"

Matt stared at them. He was going to have to come clean. There was no other way. Autumn was still insisting that she didn't want to go public with their relationship, but these guys weren't the public; they were his friends, his bandmates.

West caught up with them and gave him a sympathetic smile. "Leave him alone, guys. We're all entitled to a private life, aren't we?"

Lance nodded grudgingly, but Levi narrowed his eyes at West accusingly. "You know about this mystery girlfriend, too, don't you?"

West shrugged.

"Guys, guys …" Matt held up a hand. "I'm sorry. I should have told you sooner."

"Damned straight, you should." Levi was pissed.

Lance nodded, and if anything, Matt was more bothered by the way he looked—he wasn't mad; he looked disappointed. Matt supposed he had a right to be. They'd been friends for years. They'd worked together, lived together at one point, they used to share everything.

"I wanted to tell you, but …"

"But what?" Levi scowled at him. "Why was it okay to tell Elle and Tasha who you've known for five minutes, but not us, your friends who you've known for years? We've always had your back—what is it? You don't trust us all of a sudden?"

Matt put at hand on his shoulder. "Give it up, bud. It's not like that, and you know it. Autumn wanted us to keep this a secret for a while. She needed time to get used to the idea, and I want to do whatever it takes to help her get used to it. The only reason I told Elle was because she thought she … you know … she was interested. So, I had to tell her that I was already seeing someone; I just couldn't tell her who."

Levi and Lance were both staring at him open-mouthed.

Lance recovered first. "Damn! Although, it does make sense of a few things."

"What things?" asked Matt.

Lance smiled. "You two haven't screamed at each other in weeks."

Matt smiled through pursed lips. Autumn had done a fair amount of screaming, but not the kind Lance was talking about—and nothing that he needed to know about.

"And that first day the girls were in the studio, Autumn came down, and when she saw you and Elle in the booth, she looked pissed. I thought she was mad about something, but then she went all mild mannered and smiley and left—that really worried me."

Matt had to laugh at that. He remembered her telling him that she hadn't enjoyed seeing him sing with Elle.

Levi sputtered and finally found his voice again. "You and Autumn?"

Matt nodded.

"Wow!" Levi shook his head. "Damn." He grinned. "Way to go, dude."

Matt had to laugh. "Thanks."

Levi nodded. "That's awesome. I mean. Just. Wow! Autumn's ..." He shrugged. "She's amazing. She's hot. She's smart. She's ... Well, damn, I'll say it; I've always thought of her as out of our league."

West raised an eyebrow at him. "Autumn's a class act, but that doesn't mean she's out of Matt's league. It strikes me that maybe you should change the way you look at things."

Levi frowned at him. "What do you mean?"

West laughed. "I mean, maybe it's time you stopped playing in the minor leagues."

Matt couldn't hold back a laugh at the look on Levi's face as Lance grasped his shoulder. "He's right, you know. Instead of chasing groupies, you could step it up and ask Paige out."

Levi's face turned white, and he shook his head rapidly. "Nah. Paige is out of my league."

Matt grinned at him. "Just like you thought Autumn was out of mine?"

Levi held his gaze for a long moment. "It's not the same. I'm happy for you. I am. I hope it works out. You two could own this town between you."

Matt shrugged. "I'm not interested in owning anything. I'm only interested in seeing where things go between us." He could hardly admit that he would love to be the guy who owned Autumn's heart. He'd already given his to her a long time ago—whether she realized that yet or not.

They all looked up as the doors at the end of the hall swung open, and Autumn came in, closely followed by Corbin.

She shot Matt a puzzled glance and then looked around at the rest of them. "Is everything okay? I thought you were running through one last rehearsal."

Matt's heart raced as he willed the others not to say anything. He'd have to tell her that he'd told them what was going on, but he didn't want Levi blurting out that he knew. "We just got done," he said with a smile. "I was on my way up to see you."

She met his gaze for a moment and nodded briefly. It was a gesture he'd grown used to over the last few weeks. He loved it. It was a like a secret signal between the two of them. Now he wondered if the others noticed it, too, and now knew what it meant.

"So, this is it, then?" asked Corbin. "You're all set, and there's nothing left to do before you leave on Thursday?"

Matt nodded. "All done."

"Great." Autumn smiled around at them. "And you're all good with the arrangements?" She held West's gaze for a moment. "There aren't going to be any issues with having the girls along?"

West gave her a rueful smile and shook his head. "We all know what we have to do."

"Good."

"How often will you be coming out to see us?" asked Levi.

Autumn shrugged and shot a quick glance at Matt. They'd talked about that just last night as they lay in bed. He'd asked—only half-jokingly—if she couldn't come on the road with them. Of course, her answer had been no, but he'd loved the look in her eyes when she told him that she'd find every excuse she could to come out and see him—because she didn't like the idea of them spending so much time apart. "I'm sure I'll be out at least a few times." She made a face at Levi. "Why? You're not planning to create problems that I'll need to come out and solve, are you?"

He smiled. "No. I just think it'd do you good to spend more time out of the office. Come and enjoy yourself with us."

She laughed. "I might just do that." She turned to Matt. "Did you want to talk to me?"

"I did. Can I buy you a coffee?"

She chuckled. "Have I ever said no to that?"

Matt took her arm and started to lead her away from the others but stopped when Corbin called after him. "That's okay, I can catch up with you later."

Shit. "Sorry." He was going to have to be more careful if he wanted to keep him and Autumn a secret. The trouble was he didn't want to, and he didn't see the point. The guys knew now. Why shouldn't Corbin know too? "Do you need me now?"

The look on Corbin's face told Matt that maybe he already knew what was going on. He smiled. "That's okay. You take care of business with Autumn while I catch up with these guys. Call me later."

"Thanks." Matt turned back to Autumn, and they made their way out into the sunshine.

Once the door had closed behind them, he slid his arm around her waist and pulled her into his side, dropping a kiss on her neck. She resisted for a moment, but as he nibbled the soft skin beneath her ear, he felt the change in her as she relaxed in his arms and sagged against him.

"We shouldn't do this here," she breathed.

He slid a hand down over her ass and squeezed hard. "I can't help it. And you know, if you would just let me tell everyone that I'm the lucky bastard who gets to be with you, then there'd be no reason to hide and no reason we couldn't do this here—or anywhere."

She blew out a sigh and stepped away from him. "I know. You're right. But I'm not ready yet."

He scowled at her. "Why not?" Things were going great between them. They'd spent almost every night together since that first time at her apartment. They were getting along better than they ever had. He was learning more about her—and loving everything that he learned. He wanted to believe that it was the same for her. He didn't get why she still wanted to keep them a secret.

She shrugged. "I don't know. I guess I don't want to have to deal with it. You know it'll mean the press will be all over you for a while. And even without them, everyone will have questions—Clay, Summer, everyone. The band …" She cast a glance at the door as if the guys might be behind it, spying on them.

Matt shrugged. "You don't need to worry about them. They already know. I just told them."

Her eyes widened "What? Why?"

"Because Elle let slip that she knew that I was seeing someone, and the guys were pissed at me that she knew something they didn't. I felt bad enough anyway. I wasn't going to lie and make up someone that I'm seeing. West had an idea from the start anyway—he could see what was going on when we came back from Seattle. Lance and Levi deserve to know."

He waited for her to speak, expecting her to be angry. She didn't say anything.

"I want to say I'm sorry. I know you want to keep this secret but …" He tucked his fingers under her chin and made her look up into his eyes. "… I don't want to keep us secret. I want to tell the whole world, and I'm not sorry for telling the guys. I can't spend the next four months living in such close quarters with them and lie to them the whole time."

She nodded slowly. "You're right."

He chuckled. "Can you say that again while I record it?"

She made a face at him. "No. You won't hear me say that very often—"

"Don't I know it."

She slapped his arm and gave him a rueful smile. "I'm trying to apologize here. I might just give up if you keep making it so difficult."

He batted his eyelashes at her. "Sorry, baby girl. Go on."

She blew out a sigh. "You're right. The guys should know. I'm glad you told them. That'll make life easier when I come out to see you."

He nodded. "And when I come back to see you."

She frowned. "You don't need to do that. I can ..."

"I know you can. But you need to understand that you don't get to call all the shots on this. Yeah, I'm still your artist, and you get a say in what your artists do. But now, I'm also your man. And if you're always telling your man what to do, he'll end up feeling like not much of a man at all." He held her gaze, wondering how she'd take that. She was used to calling all the shots, and he didn't mind that so much when it came to his career. He loved that she was strong and decisive, but he wasn't signing up to be her lap dog, or her doormat.

To his relief, she smiled. "Okay."

He raised an eyebrow. "What is?"

"Everything you said. I don't know how to walk the line between treating you as my artist and treating you as my man. If this is going to work, I need you to step up and be my man—help me through this, help me figure out how to handle it."

He nodded. "I intend to. And I have to warn you that the time is coming when I'll be insisting that you stop hiding. I didn't mind being patient with you while you got used to the idea, but you've had time. I want to tell the whole freaking world. And you not wanting to is wearing thin."

"Give me a little bit longer?"

"How much longer? What are we waiting for?"

She shrugged. "It's hard to explain. I feel like in order to do what I need to do in my job, to be respected by the people in this industry, I need to be cold and hard. I don't know how to be what I need to be in my job while at the same time being what I need to be for us to work."

"What do you need to be for us to work?" Matt thought he knew what she meant, but he wanted to hear her say it.

She smiled up at him. "Open and vulnerable. Soft. I've let you through my hard, outer shell, but I don't know how I'd do my job without it."

"Maybe you don't need it?"

"Maybe—but maybe I don't know who I could be without it; not at work."

They sprang apart when the doors flew open beside them and Lance came out brandishing a magazine.

He looked at Matt, then Autumn, then back again wildly. "Err, guys … I, err … Can I have a word, Matt?"

Autumn made a face. "You can say whatever you need to say in front of me."

Lance shot an uncomfortable glance at Matt.

"It's okay." Autumn gave him a rueful smile. "I know that you know what's going on between us, and I apologize for keeping it from you guys."

Lance smiled at her. "No need to apologize. I understand, and besides, your business should be your business, but that's what I wanted to let you know." He waved the magazine at them. "It doesn't look like you're going to be able to keep it secret much longer."

Matt groaned when he saw his face smiling back at him from the cover along with the headline. *Matt McConnell's secret lover — who is she?* He looked at Autumn, wondering how she'd react. To his relief, she shrugged.

"It's my own fault, I guess. I shouldn't have tried to hide it in the first place."

Lance smiled at her. "If I were you, I'd make the most of it. Let them keep guessing for a while. The timing is great, coinciding with the beginning of the tour. It'll get more coverage while they speculate who it might be."

Matt wanted to punch him. "Or we could just come clean," he suggested. But he could tell it was too late. Autumn liked Lance's idea better and was going to run with it. Great.

Chapter Sixteen

Autumn stared at her computer screen but couldn't focus on the email she was supposed to be writing. All she could think about were the articles that had been all over the internet and the papers since that first story had run on Tuesday morning. *Who was Matt McConnell's secret lover?* She couldn't help but smile. She was. And she was thrilled to be, if she was honest. So, why wasn't she being honest? Why was she still insisting that they shouldn't come clean yet?

She blew out a sigh. She knew why. She tried to tell Matt why, but she wasn't sure he really understood. She was afraid that it would make her seem weak. She didn't have much respect for women who lost their shit over country music stars. In her mind, it was too cliché. A good-looking guy with a great voice, good looks, and a hot body could charm the pants off most women. She didn't want to be like most women. She didn't consider herself to be. She was stronger and smarter than most—tougher. She wasn't the kind to get her head turned around by fame and good looks. To be fair, that wasn't what turned her head about Matt anyway. She couldn't deny the good-looking part, but what attracted her to him wasn't his fame or celebrity status, but his character, his fun-loving, down-to-earth, kind-hearted, genuine character. She wouldn't mind the world knowing that, but she was afraid that she'd be perceived as just another woman who'd fallen for the charms of a star.

She looked up at the sound of a knock on her door. "Come in," she called.

Bianca smiled and held up two cups of coffee as she walked in. "I need to talk to you, and I thought these might help. Do you have time?"

"Sure. What's up?" She took the cup that Bianca offered and took a sip—strong and black. Unfortunately, she knew that was what Bianca brought her when they had a difficult discussion ahead.

Bianca took a seat across the desk from her and gave her a grim smile. "I need to know how you want to play this whole secret lover thing Matt has going on. I talked to him, and he insists that he just wants to ignore it for now. No comment is all he has to say. I can respect that, but you know we're missing out on a great opportunity."

Autumn stared at her over her coffee cup.

"What?" Bianca asked eventually. "Why are you looking at me like that? Do you know something I don't?" Her expression changed to one of eager curiosity. "Do you know who he's seeing?"

Autumn considered it for a few moments and then nodded slowly.

"But you're not going to tell me?"

She'd been about to. She really should tell Bianca—as a friend if nothing else. Instead, she sighed. "Not yet."

"Okay, then. If you know and you still support him in keeping it quiet for now, then I guess there's nothing else for me to say or do, is there?"

"Nope. Not yet. Let's just give it a bit more time."

"Okay. The media is having fun with it anyway. We're getting coverage just from all the speculation. We're not missing out completely."

"That's true."

"Do you think he'll come clean at some point during the tour? I'd love to capitalize on it."

"I'd say he probably will." Autumn thought about it. "And if he does, I'd also say we'll get some good mileage out of it." She knew that it would be good for the label, but she wasn't so sure how she felt about what it would mean for her.

Bianca nodded. "Okay, then. You know I'll bow to your judgment."

"Thanks."

Bianca smiled. "Is she a big name?"

"She's a name, but not a big celebrity or anything."

Bianca couldn't hide her disappointment. "Ah. I was hoping …"

Autumn gave her a rueful smile. "Don't worry, you'll still get your mileage out of it."

"Are you sure you can't tell me?"

She drew in a deep breath; she really should come clean. At that moment her phone rang, and she glanced at the display. It was Summer. "I should take that."

"Okay." Bianca got up. "But I feel like you almost cracked there. I'm going to keep working on you."

Autumn smiled and nodded but didn't say anything as she picked up her cell phone.

"Hey, sis."

"Hey, Autumn. How are you?"

"I'm okay. Dealing with the usual craziness here. How about you? How are you? How are Carter and little Penny?"

"We're wonderful, thanks. All's well in our little world."

"Good. I'm glad to hear it. What can I do for you?"

Summer laughed. "You don't need to do anything for me. I just wanted to check in with you. Have a chat. You know, see how you're doing."

"Yeah. Like I said, I'm okay. Just the usual craziness here. Nothing out of the ordinary." She felt bad that she still hadn't told Summer what was going on between her and Matt.

"Only the usual craziness? I thought it might have ramped up a little given all the stories flying around about Matt."

Autumn pursed her lips.

"What? You don't have anything to say? I thought you'd enjoy bitching about how he's making your life difficult."

"Yeah." Summer was right. Normally she did have a lot to say when Matt's escapades made the press. She could hardly blame him this time, though.

"Oh, no. Does it bother you? Are you sad that he's seeing someone? Do you know who she is?"

She really should tell her sister. Summer had harped on for years that she and Matt would get together some day. "I know who she is."

"And you don't like her?"

Autumn had to laugh. There was no reason not to tell her. Summer would never breathe a word. "Actually, I do like her. She and I are quite close."

"Oh, that must be tough. He's seeing one of you friends?"

"No. He's seeing me."

"What?"

"You heard."

"Oh, my goodness, Autumn! That's wonderful. I'm so happy! I knew the two of you would end up together. What's happened? You have to tell me everything. Why are you keeping it a secret? Is it just a publicity stunt?"

"No. We were trying to keep it a secret from everyone, not just the press."

"Why? Wait a minute. How long have you been seeing each other? Have you been keeping it a secret from me?"

Autumn blew out a sigh. "We've been seeing each other for a few weeks now."

"So, why haven't you told me yet?"

"Because ..." Autumn stared out the window, wondering what the answer to that question really was. "I don't know, sis."

"Well, think! I need to know. I want to be happy for you, but it worries me that you don't want people to know. Why not?"

Autumn examined her nails. She'd chipped one this morning and would need to get them done very soon.

"Talk to me!"

"Okay! I like him. You were right. Happy?"

"Yes, but not completely. What's the hesitation?"

"When was the last time I was in a relationship?"

"Umm, I don't really remember."

"Yeah, me neither. Because I don't like getting close to people. I admit—as if you didn't already know—I've always liked Matt."

"Yay! Finally, you can admit it."

"But come on, Summer, think about it. I'm not good at relationships. I don't like letting anyone get close. Of all the people I could finally let get under my skin, Matt is probably the worst choice of all."

"Why? He's lovely!"

"Yes, he is, but he's McAdam Records' biggest star. Not only do we work together, but a large part of the success of the label rides on his shoulders—the rest rides on mine. What happens when it all goes wrong? That's even without talking about how I'm supposed to remain professional."

"There's nothing unprofessional about it. And who says it's all going to go wrong? Have you considered what might happen if it all goes right? The two of you could end up together and that would only take the label from strength to strength. Even if you do break up, he's such a good guy and he cares too much about Clay and the label to let it affect anything."

"You sound just like him. That's pretty much what he said."

"Because he's a smart guy. If we're both telling you the same thing, don't you think it might be worth listening to?"

Autumn sighed. "I suppose so."

"So, what else is holding you back? There's something more, isn't there?"

"Yeah."

"So, tell me."

"I can't be the cold, hard-hearted bitch who gets stuff done when I'm around him. He makes me soft."

"Aww. Sorry, but that just makes my heart melt. Why would that be a bad thing?"

"Because I still have a job to do—and I need to be the cold bitch to get it done. You know what it's like in this town. You of all people know that …" She stopped. She'd been about to say that soft-hearted people didn't make it too far in the industry. She didn't finish the sentence, but Summer knew what she meant.

"I think you're wrong about that. I did just fine. I know you ran interference for me, but even by myself, I didn't get chewed up and spat out. Your heard-hearted act isn't as necessary as you think it is. People respect you because of your intelligence and your ability to get things done. They don't respect you because they fear the bitch."

Autumn thought about that. "Maybe not, but wouldn't they lose respect for me if I'm just another sappy female who fell for a big-name singer?"

Summer laughed. "You're not serious, are you? The whole world loves a love story. I think you're seeing it all wrong. I don't think anyone would lose respect for you; I think they'd gain some. It takes more strength and courage to follow your heart and let yourself fall in love than it does to hide behind the armor of a tough-girl exterior."

"Ouch."

"Well, I'm sorry, but it's true."

Autumn didn't say anything for a good few moments, then she asked, "Is that really what you think I've been doing? Hiding?"

"You said it yourself last time you were here. You have to put on the tough outer shell to deal with the world you work in. I understand it, but yeah, it is a form of hiding and keeping yourself safe."

"I'm not a coward."

"No, I know you think it's just the most efficient way—and up to now it has been. But if staying behind that tough shell means that you don't get to be the real you—the softer you, the girl who can be brave enough to fall in love with Matt—then I think that would be a real shame."

"Who said anything about falling in love?"

Summer laughed. "You didn't need to. Does Clay know?"

"No."

"Don't you think you should tell him?"

"Yeah, but I don't want to."

"What, because you think he'll think less of you—see you as weak somehow?"

"I dunno."

"It takes a different kind of strength to be brave enough to fall in love, Autumn. Clay's learned that for himself. He'll be thrilled for you, I promise. I really think you should tell him."

Autumn nodded slowly. This conversation was a wake-up call. She'd been trying to convince herself that she was keeping her and Matt a secret for some logical reason. Now, she could see, even if she hated to admit it, that all she was doing was biding her time because she was afraid.

"Are you going to say anything?" asked Summer.

"Thanks," she muttered grudgingly.

Summer chuckled. "You're welcome, and I hope the day comes sooner rather than later when you can see the truth in what I'm saying, and you'll say thanks and mean it."

Autumn had to smile. "I already do, but you know how much I like being wrong."

"You weren't wrong, you were just learning."

"Whatever. I'm going to go now. I have work to do and it seems I have some thinking to do about how I move forward with this."

"Okay. I'll let you go, but you don't need to think too hard; in fact, I'd suggest you stop thinking about it and just get on and live it."

"You're probably right."

"I know I am, but I'm not going to push it—as long as you promise to call me soon."

"I will."

"Okay, bye then. I love you, sis."

"Love you, too."

Autumn hung up and stared out the window at the city skyline. If Summer was right—and she kind of knew she was—what would that mean? Should she just come out and admit to the industry and the world that she was the one who Matt was seeing—that they were an item and that ... no she wasn't ready to mention the L word. It was way too early to mention that. Or was it? She blew out a sigh and turned back to her computer screen. She had work to do; she could ask herself that question later—on her own time.

Matt picked up his phone and then set it down again. He had the bus to himself, and he wanted to talk to Autumn so badly, but he'd been calling her so often that he felt like he was starting to make a pest of himself. She was always happy to hear from him and happy to talk to him, but so far, she hadn't called him. He wasn't being petty—at least, he didn't think he was—but he'd decided to wait and see how long it took her. He felt like things were going great between them—apart from that little detail of her still wanting to keep them a secret—but maybe he was just fooling himself? Maybe he was getting carried away with how he felt about her and wasn't paying attention to the feedback on how she felt about him. If he stopped and thought about it for too long, it worried him a little. She still didn't want anyone to know about them. He was the one doing all the running; she wasn't calling him. He knew in his heart that he was in love with her. She hadn't done anything to indicate that she felt the same way. He could be patient, if that was what she needed, but what he didn't want to do was rush them both to a place where she didn't even want to go. Maybe she never would feel the same way about him as he did her, and if that was the case, he'd have to accept it.

He turned his phone over in his hands and smiled. He could start with his new approach tomorrow. Today he just needed to hear her voice. He hit number one on the speed dial and waited.

"Hey, you."

The way she answered made him glad that he'd called. Normally she said *this is Autumn* even though she must know it was him.

"Hey, baby girl. How you doing? I miss you."

She was silent for a few moments, and his heart started to race as he wondered what she was going to say.

She sighed. "I'm not doing so great. If I'm honest, and I think it's about time that I am, I miss you, too."

He couldn't help the big grin that spread across his face. "You do?"

"I do. I don't like waking up and not seeing your face."

Wow. This was new. She hadn't talked like this before, and he loved it. "I'm the same. As soon as I open my eyes, I look over at the other pillow, but you're not there, and then I remember."

"It sucks, doesn't it?"

He nodded happily to himself, thrilled if a little shocked that she felt the same way and more so that she was admitting it. "It does. What do you think we should do about it?"

"I was thinking I could meet you in Atlanta on Friday."

Matt's heart leaped. "I'd love that. How long can you stay?"

"I was thinking the whole weekend, maybe even Monday, too."

Wow! That was longer than he'd hoped for. "That'd be awesome. I'll book us a hotel, somewhere nice."

"There's no need. You've got shows Friday and Saturday nights. No one will notice if I stay on the bus with you."

Matt didn't know what to say. "I'd love that, if you're sure."

"Why not? The guys already know, and I'm getting closer to being okay with everyone knowing."

"You are?"

"Yeah."

"Mind if I ask what changed?"

She gave a low chuckle. "You have my little sister to thank. She gave me a severe talking to and basically told me that I'm just being a coward. That I need to follow my heart and deal with whatever fallout comes when it comes. There are no guarantees, right? And as much as I like to control things, this is something I have no control over."

"Damn, baby girl. You're laying it all out there for me."

"I should have done right from the start."

"Nah, you needed time to know if this is what you really want. Mind if I ask you a question, though?"

"Sure."

"If Summer said you need to follow your heart, am I allowed to hope that your heart is getting involved here?"

She was quiet long enough that he began to regret asking, but his own heart raced when she finally answered.

"You don't need to hope. You can know without a doubt that my heart is involved. Not just involved, it's way out if its depth in uncharted territory."

He smiled. "I'll be happy to guide it if you like."

"I'm counting on it."

That almost took his breath away. She was counting on him? That was something she'd told him many times over the years that she could never do. "I won't let you down."

"I know."

Chapter Seventeen

By the time Friday rolled around, Autumn couldn't wait to leave the office and fly out to Atlanta to meet Matt. She missed him so much it felt like a physical ache deep in her chest. She wished that she'd announced her plans earlier in the week, but it was too late now. Clay and Marianne were arriving this morning, and since they didn't know she was headed to Atlanta, Marianne had invited her to lunch, and Clay wanted to meet with her afterward.

She looked up at the clock on the wall. It was eleven fifteen; they should be here within the hour. Just as she turned back to her computer, there was a knock on the door, and it opened.

Clay stood there smiling at her, and Marianne waved at his side.

"Are you busy, little girl? We got in early."

She smiled and got to her feet. "I'm never too busy for you guys, you know that." She greeted Clay with a peck on the cheek and then allowed herself to relax in Marianne's embrace for a moment. There was something about the older woman that made Autumn feel at home. She was the kind of mother figure Autumn had never known. Her own parents weren't big on showing physical affection—or any kind of affection. They weren't even big on keeping in contact with their daughters.

Marianne stepped back and looked her over with a smile. "You're looking well. You know I worry about you working so hard, but I have to say that it seems to be doing you good."

"Thanks."

Clay raised an eyebrow at her. "I wasn't sure how you were doing. I thought you might be stressed over this whole deal with Matt."

Her heart started to race. Did he know what was going on between the two of them? She'd been putting off telling him, but she hated the thought that he must have found out from someone else.

He cocked his head to one side. "This whole secret lover thing. The press is having a field day with it."

She nodded, relieved that he didn't know that she was the secret lover but feeling guilty as hell that she should tell him.

"Yeah, it's not ideal, but I think we've got it under control for now."

"What's he thinking?" asked Clay. "I've tried calling him a few times, but he hasn't returned my calls. I know it gets crazy out on tour, but I can't help feeling like he's avoiding me. Do you know what's going on? Do you know who this mystery woman is?"

Autumn stared at him. She should just come out and tell him, but with the two of them staring at her like that, it was just too much.

Clay took her silence to mean that she didn't know and wasn't happy about it. He shook his head sadly. "That worries me. If he hasn't told you and he hasn't told me, that makes me think that whoever this woman is, she's important to him. I just want to know why he's keeping quiet. Does he think we won't approve? Does he know he's making a bad choice?"

"I … I don't think that's it." Autumn had to say something to defend Matt. If it were up to him, he would have told Clay from the get-go.

Clay held her gaze for a long moment. "Do you know more than you're telling me? I thought you'd be spitting fire and totally pissed at him."

She shrugged. "Yeah, I do know a little something, but I think the situation needs a little more time yet. Let me talk to him and then he—or I—will tell you more."

"Okay. I trust your judgment. And you're going to Atlanta for the weekend, right? I take it you plan to bring him into line?"

She nodded. "Yeah. You could say that."

"How do you feel about all this?"

"What do you mean?"

Clay shook his head. "I always thought the two of you were just dancing around the inevitable, that you'd get together one day. My gut tells me that whoever he's hiding from us is someone very important to him. He wouldn't be hiding her otherwise. Are you going to be okay if he's getting into something serious?"

"Of course, I am." She had to hide a smile. The way she felt, she'd be more than happy if Matt was getting into something serious—with her. She just wanted to be sure of herself before she told Clay.

Clay chuckled. "I can only guess that he's got some kind of trouble brewed up, that you know what it is, and that you reckon you can resolve it before I need to hear about it. I've never seen you so tight-lipped about Matt. I'm more used to having to listen to you bitch about him and his antics."

She had to smile at that. "Okay, you got me. I'm sure we'll be ready to tell you all about it soon."

"Fair enough. I have you run the place so that I don't need to deal with all of this. So, I guess I can't complain if you choose to keep me in the dark." He turned to Marianne and kissed her cheek. "Do you want to call me when you ladies get done with lunch?"

Marianne smiled up at him. "Okay, but is there anything urgent you need to meet with Autumn about?"

Clay frowned. "Nothing urgent." He looked at Autumn. "Is there?"

She shook her head and looked at Marianne, wondering what she was thinking.

The older woman smiled at them. "I just thought maybe you could take me on that walk you promised me this afternoon—especially if Autumn wants to get on her way to Atlanta?"

Clay looked a little surprised, but nodded. "Sure. Whatever you want, darlin'."

He pecked her cheek and then smiled at Autumn. "I guess we can catch up after you solve your Matt problem."

"That might be better." She was grateful to Marianne for saving her from having to meet with Clay later. This way, the next time she spoke with him, she'd be ready to come clean with him about her and Matt.

Once he'd gone, she smiled at Marianne. "Where do you want to have lunch?"

"I don't mind. Wherever you want to go. All I want is to catch up with you. And if you want to unload anything, I'll happily be your sounding board—or whatever else you need."

Autumn held her gaze for a long moment. "Do you know? How do you know?"

She smiled. "I don't *know*, but I'm guessing that you're the one Matt is keeping a secret."

Autumn let out a deep breath and nodded.

"I want to say that's wonderful! I've thought the two of you would be great together ever since I met you. But, what's the problem? Why the secrecy? And especially, why not tell Clay? I can't imagine him being anything but thrilled for you. He sees you both as family."

"I know. I just … I'm being stupid, I guess. I don't want to let him down."

"Let him down?" Marianne looked puzzled. "Come on, let's go and get some lunch and you can tell me all about it."

Once they were seated in the restaurant, Marianne smiled encouragingly. "So, do you want to tell me about it, or should I just butt out?"

"I don't want you to butt out. I'm glad you know, though I'm not sure I could have made myself tell you."

"Why not? Is there some complication? Some reason that the two of you want to keep this a secret?"

"No. At least, there's nothing complicated about it outside of my head. Matt would love to tell everyone. He wanted to from the start. It's me who's been holding back."

"Why?" Marianne held her gaze for a moment. She was such a kind soul. She made Autumn feel safe in a way she wasn't used to.

"I don't really know. A thousand reasons, and at the same time, no good reason at all. I wanted to be sure of my feelings at first. I mean, come on, it's Matt. He's been a pain in my ass for years."

"But now you're sure that you feel something for him?"

Autumn nodded. "I am. Now that I've dropped my whole defensive thing, I can admit that he's a great guy. In fact, he's an amazing guy." She smiled and looked away for a moment.

Marianne touched her arm. "So why wouldn't you want Clay and your friends—or the whole world—to know that you're happy with an amazing guy?"

"Because … because. Damn. I don't even know anymore. At first, I thought it was wrong to get involved with him—because of the label. But I know I was only using that as an excuse. I also had this idea that falling in love with a guy—especially one of the artists—would make me look weak, would cost me my credibility in the industry, but Summer made me see I was wrong about that—I was just lying to myself and using that as an excuse."

"An excuse for what?"

"To be a coward and avoid laying myself open to getting hurt."

"Especially publicly?"

Autumn thought about that. "No. I'm less worried about the media coverage and about the whole world knowing than I am about Clay and our friends knowing."

"Because …?"

"Because I know this could all go wrong. I could get hurt. And if I do, I'll seem weak."

Marianne shook her head. "It's not weakness to lay yourself and your heart on the line. Even if things don't work out. There's nothing weak about opening your heart up to a man—even if in the end it gets broken."

"I can see that now. I'm wrapping my head around it; it's just taken me a little while to accept that I can still be me without the hard-shell exterior."

Marianne smiled. "Those of us who care about you can see through the hard shell anyway. It doesn't fool us."

Autumn looked at her in surprise. "It's not an act."

"Oh, I know. I didn't mean that. You're a tough cookie, and I respect that about you. But it's only one aspect of who you are. It's the side of you that you let the world see, but there's another side to you—a soft, sweet girl with a big heart, and it strikes me that that side of you is ready to come into her own. Do you mind me asking—do you even know why you've kept that part of you hidden away?"

Autumn chewed on her bottom lip. "No. I don't know. I just know that it hurts too much to let yourself love someone and get nothing back."

Marianne nodded. "A guy let you down in the past?"

She shook her head rapidly. "Not a guy. I've never given a guy the chance to get close enough to hurt me. My parents. When we were little, I wanted so badly for them to love Summer and me. Summer's always been so soft and sweet, and she was always so hurt when they brushed her off. I tried to shield her from the hurt, but I couldn't—not completely. I suppose I tried to earn their love by being good at everything—but that didn't work either, they just weren't interested in us. I learned to not care so much. It was harder for Summer because she's so soft; she couldn't help but care."

"So you hid away the soft Autumn and tried to keep her safe, but she's tired of hiding away. If I had to guess, I'd say Matt is the right guy to help her find her way in the world. I can't think of any other man who could support that side of you while still being strong enough to stand up to your stronger side."

Autumn chuckled. "I think you're right there. He can do both. He's so sweet—but he doesn't take my crap."

Marianne laughed with her. "And for years that's driven you crazy, but now you're ready to see him as a partner—and a partner's no good to you if they won't call you on your crap."

Matt paced up and down in the lobby of the general aviation building. Corbin had wanted him to stay at the bus and send someone to pick Autumn up. He knew what was going on between the two of them now and was happy for them, but he didn't want to take any risks of getting Matt back in time to go on stage later. It hadn't been up for discussion, though. Matt hadn't seen her for over a week, and he couldn't wait any longer.

He pulled his phone out of his pocket when it beeped with an incoming text. He smiled. He knew she was as eager to see him as he was her, but her text was brief and to the point.

We just touched down. Taxiing off the runway now.

He tapped out a reply.

Tell Luke to put his foot down. I'm here waiting.

A few minutes later the doors slid open and Autumn came hurrying through. Matt rushed toward her but slowed when the pilots, Luke and Zack, came through behind her.

Her smile faded a little, but she looked back over her shoulder and seemed to understand his hesitation. She might understand it, but she didn't share it. She rushed straight to him and threw her arms around his neck. All his reticence disappeared as he crushed her to his chest and found her lips with his own.

She kissed him back hungrily, clinging to him as she sank her fingers in his hair. When they finally came up for air, he spotted the guys standing off to one side. Shit.

She buried her face in his chest. "I missed you."

"I missed you more, baby girl. But I think we just gave the game away."

"What?" Her head jerked up and she looked around. She smiled when she saw Luke and Zack. "That's okay. They know. They've been rooting for you all along."

He smiled. "I maybe gave them too much of a hint when we were in Seattle."

She laughed. "Maybe, but I can't say anything because I told them all about it on the way here."

"You did? Why? I mean, that's great, but what's changed?"

She looked up into his eyes, and he knew the answer before she said it. "Everything."

He took hold of her hand and started to lead her toward the doors. "I like the sound of that. I want to hear all about it, but let's get out of here, can we?"

"Sure. I'm surprised Corbin let you come. We need to get you back and ready to go on."

"Corbin wasn't exactly thrilled. But it wasn't as though he could stop me, and you let me worry about getting back in time. Right now, all I want is to be with you; just a few minutes alone with my woman while she tells me what's changed and how."

He led her to the rented Ford he was driving, and she raised an eyebrow at him. "You ditched Sean?"

"I don't need a driver, and I sure as hell didn't need anyone else along with me for this reunion." He opened the passenger door and gestured for her to get in before running around to the driver's side. Once he was in, he leaned across and slid his fingers into her hair, pulling her closer so he could kiss her again. He couldn't get enough of her soft lips, and exploring her with his tongue only made him want to explore the rest of her, too.

Eventually, he lifted his head and looked down into her eyes. "Want to tell me about it?"

She let out a soft laugh. "I can tell you that it took my breath away, maybe stole my senses. I can tell you that's it's addicting and that I want more."

He laughed. "I meant tell me what's changed—not tell me about the kiss."

"I know, but it was so good that I had to tell you about it."

Wow. It seemed things really had changed. He hadn't seen her like this before, and he liked the change. "That makes me happy."

"You make me happy." She reached over and rested a hand on his thigh. "But I think maybe we should talk while you drive. We'll make Corbin and a whole stadium full of people very unhappy if we don't get you back on time."

He leaned over and stole another taste of her lips before he turned the key in the ignition. "Okay. We'll get going, but please tell me what changed?"

She smiled. "I told you that Summer called me out for being a coward. Well …" She paused and frowned. "A couple of other people have done the same thing, and it's finally gotten through. I was trying to keep us a secret because I've spent my life being afraid. I didn't want to expose myself to the world as a weak, emotional female."

He glanced across at her as he pulled out of the parking lot.

"Now I finally understand that there's nothing weak about being brave enough to take the risk to fall in love."

His heart leaped into his mouth and he pulled the car over. He turned off the engine before he looked her in the eye. "Is that what you're doing?" Even to him, his voice sounded shaky.

She nodded and gave him a small smile. "It is. In fact, I'd go so far as to say that I already have."

He cupped her face between his hands and landed a kiss on her lips. "Damn, baby girl. I've been in love with you for so long. I thought it'd take me years before you might feel the same way."

She put her hands on his shoulders and her eyes twinkled as she looked at him. "What are you saying, McConnell?"

"I'm saying that I love you, Autumn. I love you with all my heart and soul."

She pressed her cheek into the palm of his hand. "And I'm saying that I love you, too, Matt."

His heart battered against his ribcage. He'd daydreamed about hearing her say those words for almost as long as he'd known her. "Tell me again," he said with a smile.

She laughed. "I love you."

He shook his head in disbelief. "One more time."

She cupped his face and looked deep into his eyes. "I love you, Matt. I have to tell you, this is new territory for me, and I might not be very good at it, but I love you, and I want to make this work."

He closed his arms around her and held her close. "I'm glad it's new to you, and I have no worries. You're good at everything you do. If you want us to work, then I know we will." He reluctantly let go of her. "I still want to hear more about what's changed, but we need to get going."

She winked at him. "I know. I'm starting to get twitchy here about not making you late, but there was no way I was going to spoil that moment by telling you to hurry back to work."

He had to laugh. "That's good to know. And see, left to my own devices, I won't let you down."

"I know."

Chapter Eighteen

By the time they got back to the stadium they only had an hour before Matt would need to get ready. Autumn felt self-conscious when they got out of the car and he took her by the hand as they walked to his tour bus.

He glanced at her and held her hand tighter as she made to pull away. "Everyone here knows."

She frowned. "Everyone?"

She had to laugh as he hurriedly let go. "Shit! They don't, do they? You've got my head all turned around. The guys know, Corbin knows. That's about it." He held her gaze for a moment. "When can everyone know?"

It was a fair question. She'd told him she was okay with it, so why did they need to keep the secret any longer? "I suppose my only hesitation now is that I think we should tell Clay first, and I think we should tell him ourselves. I felt horrible when I saw him this afternoon and I didn't tell him."

Matt frowned.

"What?"

"I dunno. I guess I was getting carried away with the fact that you're okay with people knowing now, but we're not there yet, are we? Just a few hours ago you weren't okay enough with it to tell Clay."

"I wanted to." She smiled. "And then I talked to Marianne and she helped me work through it."

"You didn't mind telling her, but you wouldn't tell Clay?"

"She guessed. I wouldn't have told her."

"Ah, okay. That makes more sense." They reached his bus and he opened the door for her to go inside. "What did she say that changed things for you?"

"It wasn't so much what she said as what she helped me realize." She shrugged. "Stuff about my parents and how that affected me."

He came to her and put his arm around her shoulders. His eyes were filled with concern. "What stuff?

"Nothing horrible. You know what they're like. They're not interested. I loved them so much. I wanted so badly for them to love us back, and they just didn't. I guess I've built my adult life around avoiding that kind of hurt and rejection."

"I'll do my best to never hurt you, and you know I won't reject you."

He closed his arms around her waist and drew her to him. Her arms slid up around his neck. "I know. I trust you. Even if we don't work out—"

He put a finger to her lips. "Don't talk like that. We're forever, you and me."

She had to swallow around the lump in her throat.

"I mean it, baby girl. This is it. You're my woman, my lady, my baby girl, and my kick-ass bitch. You're everything to me. If you'll let me, I want to spend the rest of my life showing you how much I love you."

She nodded and had to blink away the tears that pricked behind her eyes. He hugged her close to his chest and planted a kiss on the top of her head. "I love you."

She breathed in the scent of him. "I love you, too, Matt."

His hands slid down and closed around her ass. "Want me to show you how much?" He started walking her toward the bedroom at the back of the bus.

She raised an eyebrow. "Don't you have more important things to do right now?"

He dropped his head and nibbled her neck. "What could be more important than this?"

Shivers raced down her spine, and she honestly couldn't think of anything more important than getting naked with him right now. She took a deep breath. "How about more pressing? You're playing to a packed venue in just a few—"

His hands tightened around her ass cheeks and he rocked his hips against hers. "I can't think of anything more pressing than this." His hard-on pressed into her belly, making her close her eyes against the ache between her legs.

He was right. Getting on stage in time was his responsibility, not hers. She slid her hands under his shirt and ran them over his hard abs and up over his chest. "Neither can I," she breathed.

He backed her all the way into the bedroom and closed the door behind them with his foot before turning around to make sure it was locked. When he turned back to her, he let his gaze travel over her, heating her skin just as surely as if he'd touched her with his hands.

"I know we should wait," he breathed. "We don't have enough time. But I can't wait."

She shook her head and pulled his shirt up and over his head. "I don't want to wait. I want you now, Matt."

His eyes darkened with lust at her words and he pushed her skirt up around her waist. She thought he was going to push her down on the bed, but he turned her around and sat her on the little dressing table instead. She fumbled to unfasten his jeans as he opened her shirt and smiled when he saw her lacy bra. He unhooked the front fastener and dropped his head to tease her nipples with his tongue when her breasts spilled free.

She pushed down his jeans and shorts and wrapped her legs around his, sitting on the very edge of the dressing table and opening herself wide for him. "We'll have time for that tonight, Matt," she breathed and closed her fingers around him, stroking herself with the very tip of him.

He didn't lift his head, sucking hard on the taut peak of nipple and sending electric currents racing through her.

She let out a low moan. "Fuck me, Matt."

His head came up at that. "Come again?"

She chuckled. "I'm hoping to. Fuck me."

He grasped her hips. "Your wish is my command." He watched her breasts heave as she drew in a deep breath in anticipation. "And I can play with those babies again later?"

She smiled through pursed lips. "You can do whatever you want with them tonight."

He ran his tongue over his bottom lip before he bit down on it and rocked his hips, pushing at her entrance and making her whole body hum with need to feel him inside her.

"Bring on the night," he breathed as he thrust hard.

She bit off a scream as his hot, hard shaft filled her. His fingers dug into her ass, spreading her wide to receive him as he rocked his hips and pounded into her over and over, each thrust stretching her as he plunged deeper. She clung to his shoulders and moved with him, their bodies joining together, frantically becoming one as they carried each other away. The pressure started to build low in her belly. She tried to slow down, to take her time, to wait for him, but he relentlessly drove deep inside her, giving her no respite from the pleasure that started to course through her. She gasped and moaned as her muscles spasmed around him and still his hips thrust wildly. "Matt ... Matt ... Matt!!!" She screamed as her orgasm tore through her, then screamed again as he found his release and crushed her to him as he spilled his desire deep inside her.

When their bodies finally stilled, she rested her head against his shoulder. "Damn, we're good," she breathed.

He laughed. "The best, but that doesn't mean we shouldn't practice every day for the rest of our lives."

She laughed with him. "Every day and every night."

He cupped her breast and rolled her nipple between his finger and thumb, sending a delicious aftershock racing through her. "Bring on the night," he said again with a wink.

She couldn't wait.

~ ~ ~

When Matt walked out on stage a little over an hour later, his knees were weak. He always felt a thrill walking out in front of a packed stadium. He loved it. Tonight, though, the adrenaline coursing through his veins had less to do with the thousands of people screaming at him from beyond the spotlights and more to do with a single woman who stood in the wings smiling at him. He raised his hands at the crowd, and they went wild, but they weren't the cause of the buzzing in his chest and his head. That buzz was caused by the thought of Autumn—that single woman. And by the fact that he didn't want to be single anymore. He glanced over at her again, and she blew him a kiss. She felt it, too; he knew she must, or she wouldn't look the way she did right now. Yeah, of course, she had that freshly-fucked glow about her—and knowing that he was the one who'd given it to her was a high of its own. But the way she looked at him, she was all soft and sweet, and the way she blew him that kiss, not caring who saw. It told him all he needed to know. She was a woman in love—in love with him, and he was going to make her his wife.

He launched into the first song, and Levi leaned in beside him, strumming his guitar and driving the women in the audience wild. Tonight was a good night; maybe the best night of his life so far. He had the woman he loved here with him, his friends and bandmates making great music with him, and a stadium full of adoring fans loving everything they did.

As they launched into the second song, he glanced over at Autumn again. In a moment or two, Elle would come over to share his mic. Every night so far, the crowd had loved that moment—and he'd endured it, knowing what the world was thinking and wishing that he could tell them the truth. That Elle wasn't the woman he wanted by his side.

He frowned when he couldn't see Autumn. The place where she'd been standing was empty, but a few feet farther away, Corbin stood looking anxious.

When they finished the fourth song, Matt ran off stage to change his shirt. He looked around wildly for Autumn, but there was no sign of her.

Corbin came and handed him a towel.

"Do you know where she went?"

Corbin shrugged. "She's around somewhere."

Matt nodded. He'd been hoping to sneak a kiss, but there was no time. He had to get back out there.

It was going on eleven by the time they finished the closing number. He'd only caught sight of Autumn a couple of times. She'd smiled and waved when he caught her eye, but the magic that had buzzed between them during that first song was gone. He grabbed a bottle of water as he came off stage and looked around for her. She was talking on her cell phone behind one of the monitors. He hurried over to her.

She looked almost guilty when she saw him approach. "I'll call you in the morning. Hopefully, nothing will come of it … okay … bye."

She hung up and smiled at him. "Great set. They loved you out there."

He frowned. She sounded like the old Autumn, congratulating her artist on a good performance while still distracted by other problems.

He slid his arms around her waist. "Thanks, but I'm more concerned about you loving me back here."

She smiled and rested her head against his chest for a moment before looking up into his eyes. "I do." She searched his face for a moment. "I always will. But maybe we were getting ahead of ourselves. Maybe we should slow it down and see how realistic we're being."

His heart raced. "What do you mean? Why? What changed?"

She shook her head. "Nothing. I'm sorry. Nothing changed. It's all okay." She smiled again, but it looked forced. "Do you want to get a drink with everyone?"

"No. I don't. I can do that every night for the next few months. I want to go back to the bus with you and remind you just how realistic this is."

She looked as if she was about to argue, but then her expression softened, and she nodded. "Yeah. We should make the most of the time we have."

He should have been pleased by that, but something about the way she said it worried him.

When they got back to the bus, he closed the door and locked it behind them. "Who were you talking to back there?"

"Just Bianca."

"What's the problem?"

She made a face. "Nothing—yet."

"Want to tell me about it?"

"No. I really don't." She came toward him and unbuttoned his shirt before pushing it off his shoulders. "I think we should get you in the shower."

Part of him wanted to argue, wanted to make her tell him what Bianca had wanted and why she was so different when he came off stage than she'd been when he went on, but that part of him couldn't make itself heard when she started taking her own shirt off. And when she unfasted her bra and set her breasts free, that part of him couldn't even remember what it had wanted to say.

When he woke up the next morning, he opened his eyes and smiled when he saw her. She was so damned beautiful. She was in love with him. He was in love with her, and if it were up to him, before long, she'd be his wife. He let his imagination run wild with that one as he lay there somewhere between asleep and awake. Who would he ask to be his best man? He'd like to ask Clay, but he wasn't sure. Clay had given Summer away at her wedding. He was like a father to the girls, maybe Autumn would want him to give her away, too? He didn't see how he could ask one of the guys—it wouldn't go over well with the others. Maybe Corbin? He opened his eyes and watched her sleep beside him. It didn't really matter who stood beside him at the altar, only that she joined him there and that she said yes to being his wife. He wondered how long he should wait. How soon was too soon? As far as he was concerned, tomorrow would be just fine—hell, today would be better. But she'd need more time. This time yesterday she hadn't even been ready to admit to Clay that they were seeing each other. Yeah, she'd need more time, and he'd give her as much as she wanted. He rolled onto his side and brushed a strand of hair away from her face. He'd give her all the time in the world. He'd give her all the days of his life if she'd let him. Whether he spent those days married to her or waiting to get married to her didn't matter so much as long as she'd say yes when he asked.

She opened her eyes and smiled at him. "Good morning."

"Good morning, beautiful." He slid his arm around her and drew her close to him, loving the feel of her naked breasts pressed against his chest. "What do you want to do today?"

Her eyes clouded over.

"What? What's wrong?"

She shook her head sadly. "Remember that call from Bianca last night?"

"Yeah."

"I should probably go back and deal with it."

He felt as though she'd punched him in the gut and involuntarily tightened his hold on her. "Don't go. Surely Bianca can deal with it. I bet she'll step up to the plate and take care of business if you give her the chance."

She made a face. "It's something I need to deal with myself."

"You think that about everything. Haven't I proved to you that I'm capable of more than you realize if you just leave me to my own devices?"

He didn't understand the look on her face. "Did I say something wrong?"

"No." She shook her head sadly. "You didn't do anything wrong at all. I just have to figure out how I'm going to deal with this—*if* I can deal with it."

"Is there anything I can do to help?" He knew there was no point trying to talk her out of it. She had to do whatever she had to do, just like he had to stay here and go on stage tonight.

"Thanks, but I don't think so."

He dropped his head and nibbled on her neck. "You don't have to go right now, do you?"

"No, but I need to call Zack and Luke and ask them to have the plane ready."

He rolled her onto her back and propped himself up on one elbow to look down into her eyes. "Can you spare me half an hour before you call them?"

He watched the struggle on her face, and his heart buzzed when she gave in and nodded. It didn't feel like too much of a victory, though. Not with the sad way she smiled at him or the way she held onto him just a little too tight when he hugged her.

"Are you sure you're okay?" he asked.

The sadness was gone when she met his gaze and laughed. She sounded more like her old self when she said, "I will be if you make this half hour worth me sticking around for."

Chapter Nineteen

Autumn pushed through the doors at the McAdam building and strode toward the elevators. She hadn't allowed herself to think about this new situation all the way back here. Matt had driven her back to the airport after their time in bed this morning. She pressed her lips together. Maybe that had been their last time in bed together. If the stories were true, she should make sure it was their last time—even if a part of her didn't want to.

She rode the elevator up to her office and slumped down in her chair. She was grateful that Matt hadn't seen the stories before she left. She wanted to figure out how she felt about it before she heard what he had to say. Her phone buzzed, and she pulled it out of her purse. It wasn't him. Maybe he hadn't seen the news yet; she found that hard to believe, though. Corbin must've seen by now, and she had no doubts he'd go straight to Matt when he did.

This was a text from Clay. She'd answer him later, just like she'd have to answer most of the other twenty-seven texts and six voicemail messages that had backed up over the course of the morning.

She looked at the clock on the wall. Bianca had said she'd meet her here at one. That gave her an hour to do some thinking. She wasn't so worried about how they could put a good spin on this from a PR standpoint. She knew they could turn it around into a positive; it was easy to do that with Matt. He was such a likeable guy, and it seemed the public always wanted to believe the best about him. What she needed the time for was to come to terms with how she wanted to handle the situation for herself. She already knew what it meant for their relationship. They were over. They had to be. He'd lied to her—even if only by omission. He'd omitted to tell her something major about himself and his life. Even if she could get past that, she couldn't get past the fact that he had a daughter. She wasn't going to break up with him over him not telling her the truth. She was going to break up with him because she didn't want to be with a guy who had a child with another woman. Maybe he'd get back together with the mother—she hoped for the child's sake that he would. Even if he didn't, he should be a part of the child's life—and she had no desire to be. Maybe that made her look selfish. So what if it did? She wasn't driven by selfish desires—only by the desire that the child should get the best parenting possible; and she was in no way ideal stepmother material. She knew it. She wasn't prepared to step into that role. Her own relationship with her parents had made her wary. She knew how badly you could screw a kid over without even trying if you weren't prepared to dedicate yourself to their well-being.

Her phone rang and she checked the screen. It was Summer. She let it ring. As soon as it stopped it started up again. She made a face. Summer was too good at this. She'd keep calling all day unless she answered or turned her phone off. She was tempted to do the latter, but on the fifth time ringing she picked up and answered instead.

"What?"

"You know full well what."

"Yeah, I do. What do you want me to say?"

"Is it true?"

Autumn wanted to kick herself. She'd been so caught off guard by the revelation that Matt had a child, and so devastated by what it had to mean for their relationship, she hadn't stopped to ask the obvious question. "Of course, it is. Everything you read on the internet is always true."

"Don't! Don't be all snappy and snarly. I'm worried about you. Is it true? What did Matt say?"

Autumn pursed her lips.

"Oh my goodness! Don't tell me you haven't asked him."

"Okay, then I won't."

"Why not? Autumn, that's crazy. If the two of you are going to get through this, you have to be able to talk to each other. Communication is everything in a relationship."

"Well, I guess I don't need to worry about it since we can't be in a relationship."

"Why not?"

"Not if he has a kid."

"Stop it. For one thing, you don't even know if he does— and I can't believe that of you. You always verify the facts before you move forward with anything. Why didn't you ask him?"

"You want to know why? I'll tell you why. I didn't ask him because last night before he went on stage I told him that I loved him; he told me that he loved me, too. He told me that he wanted to spend the rest of his life showing me just how much. We screwed each other's brains out on the bus before he went on stage. I stood in the wings feeling all sappy and stupid and finally believing in happily ever afters. Then Bianca texted me a link to the story. The photos, Matt and his cute little daughter, Matt and his baby momma and their gorgeous little girl. Just when I thought I was ready to come clean as Matt McConnell's secret lover, the press is announcing that they've discovered who she is—and that she's also the mother of his child. Forgive me for feeling too hurt to want to stick around and talk about it with him. Instead, I made out that I didn't know anything about it. I spent the night with him—because I'm that sad that I wanted to sleep beside him one more time—and this morning, we had the best goodbye sex he'll ever know." She drew in a deep breath and made herself stop.

"And poor Matt didn't even know it was goodbye?" asked Summer sadly.

Autumn sighed. "No. I didn't think he needed to. Just like he didn't think I needed to know he has a kid."

"I'm sorry. I feel bad that it hurt you so much. I hate that it's messing everything up for you just when it's starting to go right, but don't you think you should talk to him—ask him if it's even true?"

"I know damn well I should ask him. I'm not stupid. But I just had to get away from him first. If he says yes it is, I don't want to be around him. I don't want to hear his explanations, and I can't be around him when I tell him that we're over."

"Because you're afraid that he could persuade you that you're not?"

"Yeah. If I'm honest, I don't want to spend my life with a guy who already has a kid. I know a lot of people do that—and that's fine for them. But not me. I can't just flip a switch and love someone else's child with all my heart from the get-go, and I've always sworn I won't have kids until I'm ready to dedicate my life to them. I'm not going to raise my kids the way we were raised."

Summer was quiet for a long few moments.

"What?"

"I don't think there's any point in me saying."

"Say it anyway. I know you're going to tell me I'm wrong somehow."

"Okay. I think there are more options than just the two extremes. It's not a case of dedicate your whole life to your child or neglect them completely. I know with Penny, we're somewhere in the middle. She's my whole world, but she's not my *whole* world, if you know what I mean."

"Okay. I think I do, but would you let me overreact here?" Autumn was beginning to see that maybe she was being a little extreme, but she was shocked and hurt and didn't know how to handle any of this. "I'm just doing the only thing I know how to do. I don't know how to handle it, so the obvious solution is to walk away."

"It doesn't seem like much of a solution to me. And you're solving a problem that you're not even sure exists yet. You need to talk to him. Find out if it's true."

"And I will, once I'm done freaking out here."

She could hear the smile in her sister's voice. "Will you let me know how it goes?"

Autumn had to smile. She liked to think that she was the one who looked out for Summer, but she was grateful that the tables could be turned when needed—even if she hadn't known she needed it. "Okay. And thanks, sis."

"You're welcome. I'm glad you answered. I didn't think you would."

Autumn laughed. "I knew you'd wear me down by calling and calling. You can be a real pain in my ass when you get started."

"It's called persistence. I'm not a pain in the ass. I just care enough to not give up on you—even when you want me to."

"Whatever you call it. I appreciate it. Love you."

"Love you, too. Call me soon, and let me know how it goes—or I'll have to start persisting again."

"Okay. I will."

Autumn hung up and stared out the window for a few moments. She knew what she should do—she should call Matt and ask him if it was true. Her heart beat faster. If it wasn't true, why hadn't he called her? Surely, if it were just some story the press had concocted, he'd want to talk to her, reassure her. Maybe he hadn't even seen it yet? Either way, maybe it would be better to wait for him to call her?

She picked up her phone and set it down again. Yeah. She should wait. Bianca should be here soon. The two of them needed to come up with an official line—either way. They could work through the options of how the label wanted to work this if it was true—and if it wasn't.

No. That was dumb, and she knew it. She was simply looking for a way to avoid the inevitable. What she needed to do was talk to Matt. She picked up her phone again and set it down again when her door flew open, and Bianca came in.

"Hey! What did he say? Is it true?"

Autumn made a face. "I don't know."

"What? What did he say?"

"I didn't ask him."

Bianca grasped the edge of the desk and leaned toward her. "Huh? Why? You were right there with him last night. Why didn't you ask him when he came off stage?"

Autumn had to come clean. "I didn't ask him because I wasn't sure I could handle the answer."

"What do you mean? Why not? We need to know if his secret lover is the mother of his child. We need to know how we're going to handle this whole story."

"I already know that the secret lover is not the woman in the photos. What I don't know is whether that really is his child."

"How do you know she's not the one he's been hiding?"

"Because I am."

"You are? You are what? … Oh!" Bianca pulled the chair out and sat down opposite her. "You're telling me that you're the secret lover?" She recovered from her shock and laughed incredulously. "You're bullshitting me, right? You did talk to him and he wants to hide something and so you—for some unknown reason—have volunteered to be the secret woman?"

Autumn shook her head firmly. "Nope. I bullshit you not. Matt and I have been seeing each other for a couple of months now. He wanted to tell everyone; I wanted to keep it quiet until I felt more certain about us."

Bianca's eyes were wide. "You? And Matt? Together? And you didn't tell *me* because …?"

"Don't take it personally. I only told Summer yesterday. And I still haven't told Clay."

"Wow. So you're really not sure about it?"

"That's the trouble. I am now—or at least, I was until I found out that he has a daughter he hasn't told me about. It might have just slipped his mind, you know? But …"

"Or maybe he doesn't have a child at all. You know how the media works; they get a hint of something, and they decide to run with it—before they know if there's even a shred of evidence to support it."

Autumn made a face. "I know. But I'm hardly being logical about this. How would you react if a guy you were seeing suddenly had a kid that he hadn't told you about?"

"Well, unlike you, the first thing I would do is *ask* him."

"All right, all right. In my defense, I was about to call him when you walked through the door. I needed a bit of time to figure out how I felt first, but you're right, I do need to talk to him."

Bianca picked up her cell phone from the desk and handed it to her. "So, call him. I'll be in the break room, making coffee." She got up and paused when she reached the door and smiled. "And just so you know, I think the two of you will make a great couple. You're awesome together."

Autumn smiled. She thought so too. Her smile faded. She loved the idea of being part of a great couple with him, but not of being a stepmom to his child.

"You don't know if it's true yet." Bianca read her thoughts. "I'll be in the break room."

Autumn took a deep breath then dialed his number and waited.

Matt was out of the cab before it even stopped. He threw a couple of twenties at the driver and ran inside the terminal building. This might not have been his greatest idea, but he hadn't known what else to do. He'd gotten used to having Luke and Zack and the jet on call whenever he needed to get anywhere in a hurry, but they'd flown Autumn back to Nashville an hour ago. It'd take too long to wait for them to come back and pick him up. He needed to get to her, and he could only hope that he'd be able to get on a commercial flight on standby. He headed straight for the desk and put on his best *I'm-just-a-dumb-country-boy-can-you-help-me?* smile when then the woman sitting behind it greeted him.

"When's your next flight to Nashville?"

She tapped at her keyboard and checked the screen in front of her. "We have one at four o'clock and another—"

"That's too late!" He ran a hand through his hair. "I need …"

She smiled kindly at him. "Hold on." She tapped away. "Do you have any bags to check?"

"Nope. Just myself."

"Okay." She tapped again. "If we can get you through security in time, there's one boarding now."

He pulled out his wallet and handed her his credit card. "Please. Get me on it."

Another woman came out of the office behind her and did a double take when she saw him. "Oh, my Lordy. You're Matt McConnell!"

He nodded and tried to smile. "It's a pleasure to meet you. It really is. But I have to get on this plane."

The woman smiled. "Are you going to see that sweet baby girl of yours? I don't know why you kept her secret till now."

Matt stared at her. How did she know about Autumn?

The woman looked puzzled. "Or were you trying to keep her out of the limelight? I guess it must be hard to raise a child with the press always on your tail."

Matt nodded. Now he understood. She wasn't talking about Autumn. She was talking about the kid. He shrugged. He had no idea what he could say that would make the woman stop talking and all he wanted to do was make it to the gate in time before that plane took off for Nashville without him.

"What flight you trying to get him on, Audra?"

"2344 to Nashville."

The woman checked her watch and made a face. "Ain't gonna make it through security in time."

"I *have* to get on that plane," Matt said desperately.

The woman smiled at him. "Wait there." She went into the office and came back out with a wheelchair. "You sit your ass in there and let Aunt Barbie take you for a ride."

Matt looked at the wheelchair and back at her.

She smiled. "If you wanna make that plane, you gonna need a shortcut, boy."

He had to laugh. "Thanks." Audra, behind the desk, handed him back his card and a boarding pass and he sat his ass in the chair as Barbie commanded.

"Good luck," called Audra as Barbie wheeled him away.

He waved back at her with a grateful smile and made a mental note to make sure that the two of them received VIP tickets and backstage passes for the band's last night in Atlanta. Hell, maybe he'd fly them out to the final night of the tour in Seattle if they got him back to Nashville and he could work things out with Autumn.

Barbie walked him past the long line waiting at the security checkpoint. He felt like an asshole as she took him to an empty lane and the guys there patted him down and checked his boarding pass and ID. It only took two minutes to get through, and then they were on their way to the gate. There were still a couple of passengers boarding when they got there.

Matt got up from the wheelchair when she stopped and gave Barbie a hug. He couldn't help it. He felt like she'd saved his life. At least, he was hoping that she'd helped him keep the rest of it on track. He had to get to Autumn.

Barbie beamed at him. "Why, you're welcome, son. I don't know what your hurry is, but I'll be praying as it all works out for you."

He hugged her again. "Thank you. I can never thank you enough—but I'm going to try."

"Aww." She waved a hand at him. "You done thanked me enough with that hug."

"Final call," said the woman standing at the gate.

Matt showed her his boarding pass and made his way to the plane. He looked back and waved at Barbie one more time, and she blew him a kiss. That made him think about Autumn. When she'd blown him a kiss from the wings last night, he'd felt like he was on top of the world. Now he felt like his world had crumbled around him. She must have known about the pictures, about the little girl. That's what Bianca had called her about last night—it had to be. But she hadn't said anything to him. Hadn't asked him about it. That wasn't good. It meant she didn't trust him. She'd gone cold, backed off. He knew her too well; she'd closed him out. The way she'd clung to him, the sadness in her eyes this morning; it all made sense now. She'd written him off. She'd been saying goodbye to him—she just didn't want to say it *to* him.

Chapter Twenty

Autumn sat back down at her desk. She'd told Bianca to go home—get on with her weekend. They weren't going to put any kind of spin on this until she'd talked to Matt. She jumped when her phone rang. It wasn't him. She'd tried him twice, but it had gone straight to voicemail both times. She hadn't left him a message—she didn't know what she could say. She stared at the display. It wasn't Matt, but it was his agent—Corbin. She sucked in a deep breath, wondering what he had to say for himself. Her hands shook as she swiped to answer. If Matt had asked Corbin to call her instead of doing it himself …

"This is Autumn."

"Is he with you? Where the hell are you?"

"What?"

"Come on, Autumn. I know what's going on with the two of you. I understand you might have some issues to work out given the media coverage he's getting, but he can't just take off like this without telling me."

"He's not there?"

"Shit. He's not with you either?"

"I left this morning."

"Did you guys fight?"

"No."

"No?"

She sighed. "He hadn't seen anything. I didn't want to be the one to tell him that his secret was out, so I left."

"Shit, shit, shit! So, you're telling me that you don't know where he is either?"

"I have no clue. I assumed he was still there."

"Well, he's not. No one's seen him. I figured the two of you would need time to talk. I figured he'd need to explain and that … well, you guys would …"

Autumn's heart sank. If Corbin thought that Matt needed to explain the photos to her, he must know the truth. "I guess he doesn't feel the need to explain anything to me. I haven't heard from him."

"And you aren't worried?"

"I think his silence tells me all I need to know."

"Dammit, Autumn. You're as smart as they come, but when it comes Matt, you act so dumb! My guess is that the poor guy is going out of his mind with worry over what you're going to think—and do."

"My guess is that if he cared what I thought, he would have called me by now."

"Which is why the fact that he hasn't worries me so much."

Autumn frowned. "You're worried about him? I thought you were only worried about him taking off on you."

"I'm not going to lie, the thought of him not getting his ass back here in time to go out tonight worries me, but not nearly as much as the fact that we don't know where he is."

Autumn swallowed—hard. "Have you tried calling him?"

"It just goes to voicemail. I assumed that the two of you were together, so he'd probably switched it off."

"And I assumed that he didn't want to answer me."

194 SJ McCoy

Corbin made a tutting sound. "You assumed wrong. I'd put money on talking to you being right at the top of his priority list right now."

She looked up at the sound of a knock on her door. She stared at it as it swung open. Matt stood there. He didn't smile, he just stepped inside and closed the door behind him. She'd thought she knew all his looks, but this was one she'd never seen before. The lines around his eyes were etched just a little deeper. There was no cocky set to his shoulders. His smile was nowhere to be seen. He looked like he was hurting—and he looked scared.

"You can stop worrying. I found him," she told Corbin.

"Well, tell him he needs to get his ass back here by seven at the latest. And Autumn ..."

"Yeah?"

"Give him a chance to explain."

"Yeah." She hung up and met Matt's gaze. "What are you doing here? That was Corbin. He's worried."

He took a few steps toward the desk and then stopped. "Why didn't you tell me that you'd seen the story?"

"Pft!" She couldn't help the snort that escaped her lips. It took her a couple more breaths before she could speak. Her heart felt like it was shattering in her chest. She loved him; he'd finally gotten through to her. She'd finally given herself permission to relax and let him in, and now he was tearing her heart out. "Don't you think I should be the one asking you why you didn't tell me?"

He shook his head and came closer. "There's nothing to tell."

A lump formed in her throat. She wanted so badly to believe that. Part of her already did. "So what were the photos?"

He blew out a sigh. "They were just a couple I ran into at Pikes Place Market that weekend we were in Seattle. The kid was cute. The parents were cool. We snapped a few pictures. Here …" He pulled out his phone and handed it to her. There was a photo on social media of Matt, the woman, the child, and a guy. The post said:

> *Best day ever! We ran into this guy today – nicest guy you could ever meet.*
> *A big shout out to Matt McConnell for making my day and my wife's and daughter's too.*
> *Look at Evie kissing on him!*

There were several photos, including the ones that had been included with the article Autumn had seen. Below them were hundreds of comments, including a couple from Matt saying what a pleasure it had been to meet them and sending kisses to little Evie.

Autumn handed the phone back with a shaky hand.

"Do you believe me now?" His voice was deep and husky.

She nodded and tried to blink away the tears that were pricking behind her eyes. "I'm sorry."

"No! I'm sorry, baby girl. I can't imagine how you must have felt. I know it's a stretch for you to trust me—to trust in us. But I need you to know. I'll never do anything to mess this up for us. I have no skeletons in my closet. I don't have any kids—at least, not that I know of."

She had to smile at that. "That's honest."

He gave her a half smile back. "That's all I can be. I just need you to know. I love you, baby girl. I'm all in here—heart, soul, everything. You've got them, they're yours—for keeps." He came around the desk and held his arms out to her. "If you want me."

A single tear escaped as she stepped toward him. "I do want you, Matt. I want this. I was ready to run."

He raised an eyebrow at her. "Ready to? I had to chase you back here—on a regular commercial flight, in cattle class, no less."

She smiled. "Am I supposed to be impressed by the hardships you'll suffer for me?"

He held her close to his chest. "No. You're supposed to get it through your stubborn head that I am not giving up. I'll do whatever it takes. You can run if you feel the need, but you can't hide. I know what you did last night and this morning."

She tilted her head back to look up into his eyes. He planted a kiss on her lips before he continued. "You tried to shut me out, didn't you? You didn't tell me about the story. Didn't tell me what you thought you knew. You just …" He shook his head sadly. "Did you really think that you made love to me one last time before you said goodbye?"

She nodded sadly as another tear escaped.

"Well, this is me calling you on your bullshit, Autumn Breese. In the future, you have to talk to me. You have to tell me what you're thinking, and we're going to work through it together, okay?"

She nodded again.

"I know it's scary, but that's what a real relationship takes. Will you promise me that you won't shut me out like that again?"

"I promise I'll try not to."

He smiled. "At least that's honest. And it doesn't matter. I'm not going to give up on you. If you try to shut me out, I'll just keep banging down your doors till you let me back in. You know how much of a pain in the ass I can be, but if that's what it takes …"

"You sound like Summer now. And I think I finally get it. She says it's not really being a pain in the ass; it's just caring enough to not give up on me—even when I want you to."

Matt chuckled. "I always said she was the smarter sister." She slapped his arm, making him laugh again. "You know I don't mean it, baby girl. You're the smartest, most beautiful woman I ever met." He landed a kiss on her lips and murmured, "And one day soon, you're going to be my wife."

Her head jerked up, and she looked him the eye.

He grinned. "You can pretend you didn't hear that if you like, but we both know you did. I'm just putting you on notice."

She held her breath for a moment, then slowly let it out with a smile. It wasn't as though she didn't love the idea.

He slid his hands down and cupped them around her ass. "You know, every time I come in your office, I fantasize about making you come in your office."

She slid her arms up around his neck and smiled as she sat back on her desk and wrapped her legs around his. "I like the sound of this. We'll have to be quick, though; we need to get you back to Atlanta in time for the show."

He kissed her and leaned forward until she was lying back on the desk. "I'm not going unless you come with me."

She opened her eyes. "You mean here or to Atlanta?"

He smiled as he pushed her skirt up around her waist. "Both."

∼ ∼ ∼

They both scrambled to their feet at the sound of a knock on the door. Matt headed toward it to give Autumn time to straighten her clothes.

"Coming," he called as he looked back over his shoulder at her before opening it.

She winked at him and nodded as she smoothed her top down.

Matt's breath caught in his chest at the sight of Clay standing there scowling at him. "Will one of you please tell me what's going on?"

"Yeah, err, sure, err." Matt felt awful. He'd hated not telling Clay about what was happening between Autumn and him. He hated feeling like he was letting the guy down by being here right now instead of in Atlanta where he should be. And he hated that Clay had no doubt seen all the stupid drama in the gossip magazines and online.

"Come on in, Clay. I'm sorry. It's all my fault."

They both turned to look Autumn.

"What's your fault?" asked Clay.

"Nothing," said Matt. "Don't listen to her. It's all on me."

"Matt!" She frowned at him. "Don't! You wanted to come clean from the start. This is my fault."

"Stop!" Clay held up a hand. "I'm used to the two of you arguing. I get that. What I don't get is you each trying to take the blame. Normally you're blaming each other. What's going on?"

Matt looked at Autumn. He wanted to be the one to tell Clay, but he figured she might want to do it. She surprised him when she came around the desk to stand beside him. "We have something to tell you."

"No shit! I figured that much out. So, come on, what's happening? What can I do?"

Matt smiled at Autumn and slipped his fingers through hers. She lifted their joined hands to show Clay, and Matt grinned at him and said, "I finally got my girl."

Clay shook his head in disbelief and held Matt's gaze for a moment, then he looked at Autumn and nodded and smiled back through teary eyes.

"Damn!" Clay shook his head again. "I don't know what I was expecting to discover when I got here, but it sure as hell wasn't this. This is great, kids. You know I'm happy for you. Do I want to know how all this happened?"

Autumn chuckled. "Probably not."

"We wanted to work it out in our own time before we—" started Matt.

"Don't listen to him," interrupted Autumn. "He wanted to tell you right from the beginning. It was me who screwed things up by wanting to keep it to ourselves for a while. I should have come clean, then we wouldn't have had all this mess and …"

"There's not much mess," said Matt. "And you were right—" He stopped at the sound of Clay's rich, deep laugh.

"I wondered what it would be like when the two of you got together; wondered if all the bickering would stop and we'd have peace and harmony around here. I should've known better. Now you're just going to argue that the other is always right instead of them always being wrong."

Matt looked at Autumn, and they both laughed. "Probably," said Matt.

Autumn winked at Clay. "Not all the time. I still call him out when he's being a pain in the ass."

They all laughed at that. Matt knew that she would—and he wouldn't want it any other way.

"So, I don't need to worry? There are no surprise children or paternity suits I need to worry about? No missing singers?" He looked at Matt. "Do you have the guys lined up to get you back to Atlanta in time?"

Matt shook his head guiltily. That should have been his first call when he got back here, but all he'd been able to think about was getting to Autumn.

She smiled at him. "I'll get on it, now."

He couldn't resist. "I thought you didn't do travel arrangements? I thought you had staff for that?"

She reached up and landed a peck on his cheek. "I do for my artists, but I don't mind taking care of my man."

Clay grinned at him. "And on that happy note, I'm out of here." He looked at Autumn. "I take it you'll handle the media circus around this in your own time?"

She nodded. "Yeah. We'll figure out what we want to do and make it right."

"However you want to work it is fine by me. What about friends and family? Can I tell Marianne?"

Autumn gave him a sheepish grin. "She kind of knows."

Clays eyes grew wide. "She knew, and I didn't?"

Matt felt bad. "We didn't tell her, she guessed."

Autumn went to Clay and hugged him. "I hated not telling you. I just needed to work through my stuff first."

Matt had to swallow as he watched Clay hug her back. The love between them was so apparent, it drove home for him how much of a family they really were—a family that he was already a part of through his music and that he planned to become part of through marriage.

"It's okay, little girl. I know how you work. You need to be sure of yourself before you're ready to share with me. Just know, though, you'll never let me down, no matter what you do." He kept one arm around her shoulders and held the other out to Matt. "That goes for you, too, son. I love you both like you were my own. I couldn't be happier for you." He grinned at them. "But I tell you now; from here on out, I am neutral— you can fight as much as you like, but don't bring me into it."

Autumn smiled at them. "Don't worry, we won't. I can win without bringing in the big guns."

Matt laughed. "I think she means that from now on, she will meekly surrender to the will of her man."

Autumn and Clay both burst out laughing at that. "Yeah, right," said Clay. "And I'm going to catch a ride home on that flying pig. I'll see you both soon."

Once he'd gone, Matt went to Autumn and closed his arms around her, backing her toward the desk. "Where were we?"

She kissed him and then put a hand to his shoulder to push him away. "I was about to call the guys and get you set up with a ride back to Atlanta."

His smile faded. "You're not coming?"

She chuckled. "Not until we get there."

Epilogue

(Three Months Later – Seattle.)

Autumn looked out at the stadium—that was a hell of a lot of people. Matt and the band had sold out venues across the country during the four-month tour. Tonight was the final concert, and this was the biggest crowd yet. She turned when someone tapped her on the shoulder.

It was Summer. Carter stood by her side and gave Autumn that bashful smile of his.

"Hey, sis." Summer hugged her. "How are you feeling?"

"Honestly?" Autumn smiled. "Glad that it's almost over."

"I'll bet. I know Matt can't wait to get some downtime, just the two of you."

"Yeah. I'm looking forward to it." It was standard for the artists to take a couple of weeks off after a big tour. What wasn't standard was for Autumn to do the same. Matt had asked and wheedled and worked on her—she had to smile at that—until she'd finally agreed to take two weeks off with him. The tour had been a great success, but it'd been a lot of work, for both of them. The fact that they'd spent at least a few days a week together since Atlanta had been awesome, but it had meant a lot of travel. She'd gone to join him whenever she could, and he'd come back to Nashville to be with her whenever there was a break of more than a couple of days.

"Where are you going?" asked Carter.

Autumn chuckled. "I don't know. We're going to spend a couple of days here in Seattle, and then Matt just wants to go wherever the wind blows us."

Summer laughed. "Wow. It must be love. Going with the flow isn't exactly your style, is it?"

"It never used to be." She smiled. But Matt was teaching her the beauty of spontaneity.

She sensed him the moment before he slid his arms around her waist from behind and rested his chin on her shoulder.

"Hey, guys. Thanks so much for coming." He kissed her neck and then came around to hug Summer and shake Carter's hand. "I know you don't like to leave Montana much. It means a lot that you're here for us tonight."

"We wouldn't miss it for the world," said Carter.

Summer gave Autumn a weird smile. "That's right."

Autumn had to wonder why they were so enthusiastic about being here. She usually had to go and visit them because they never wanted to leave baby Penny—or come down from the mountains, for that matter. This was the last night of Matt's big tour, but she didn't think it was *that* big of a deal.

Matt seemed to think it was, though. It seemed he'd invited everyone he'd ever met. He slipped his arm through hers. "Do you mind if I steal her away?"

Summer smiled. "Of course not. We were on our way to Lawrence and Shawnee anyway." She pointed to where two of country music's biggest names were standing waving at them.

"Tell them I'll catch up with them later," said Autumn. Summer gave her that weird smile again. "I will; don't worry."

Matt pulled her to him and slid his arms around her waist as he kissed her deeply. She sank her fingers in his hair and kissed him back. She struggled at first with the way he did that when there were people around, but now she'd grown used to it—and she loved it. It was like he said—all that mattered was the way they felt about each other, not what anyone else might think.

When he lifted his head, he kept his arms around her and looked down into her eyes. "I'm thinking this is going to be the best night of my life."

She laughed. He always got pumped up for a big performance. "Good. You go out there and give it all you've got."

He stroked a strand of hair away from her face and smiled. "I plan to."

"Did you want to steal me away for something important or just for a kiss?" She checked her watch, thinking it was almost time for him to go out there.

He cupped her face between his hands. "What could be more important than a kiss?" He landed one on her lips. "You need to get your priorities straight, baby girl."

She touched his cheek. He kept doing this to her—reminding her what was really important in life. "Sorry."

He took her hand. "Don't be. Just don't ever think there's anything more important to me than us. I did want to introduce you to Barbie and Audra, though."

Autumn smiled as she followed him. He'd told her about his mad dash through the Atlanta airport to follow her back to Nashville that day. She loved that he'd invited the two women who'd helped him catch the plane in time.

Autumn smiled when she spotted them. It had to be them. She knew everyone else backstage. All the usual suspects were here. Clay and Marianne were chatting with Shawnee and Lawrence. Summer and Carter were standing with some of their friends from Montana. She wasn't surprised that Matt had invited Chance and his wife, Hope. It made her laugh how much of a man-crush Matt still had on that guy. She was more surprised that Carter's other brothers were here too. She'd gotten to know them all since Summer had moved up there. Mason, Shane, and Beau; she didn't think of any of them as the kind to want to come to a big concert, but what did she know? Maybe this was a special weekend away for them and their wives. Shane's wife, Cassidy, was one of Autumn's oldest friends. She waved when she spotted them and started toward them.

Matt tugged on her hand. "Can I just introduce you to Barbie and Audra before Cassidy gets you? I'll never get you away once she starts."

"Sure." She motioned to her friend that she'd be over soon.

"Hey, ladies. I'd like you to meet the love of my life, Autumn Breese."

The two women beamed at her. "You're even more beautiful in real life," said the older, larger woman. "It's a real pleasure to meet you."

Autumn held her hand out. "It's a pleasure to meet you, too. And I want to thank you." She smiled at Matt. "You have no idea how much you helped us when you got him on that plane."

Barbie placed both hands over her heart. "Aww, bless you, child. We're so happy to be a part of your story."

Audra smiled and nodded by her side.

Matt chuckled. "You say they have no idea how much they helped. But I've told them, and I'll tell them again—they saved the rest of my life for me."

Barbie grinned at him. "And we can't wait for—" She brought her hand up to cover her mouth and looked wide-eyed at him over it.

Matt glanced at Autumn and grinned. "They're like everyone. They can't wait to see tonight's show."

Barbie nodded. "And we don't want to make you late for it."

Autumn smiled at her. "Thanks, we should go get him ready."

Barbie grinned at Matt. "I think that boy's ready as he'll ever be."

Matt hugged her. "You know it. Stick around, won't you? We'll see you afterward."

"We'll be here waiting to congratulate you," said Audra.

Barbie glared at her and then smiled at Autumn. "We'll see you both later," she said before she dragged Audra away.

Matt slung his arm around her shoulders. "Want to come hang with me and the guys before we go out there?"

"I should let you get on. I want to find Laura and have a word with her. I haven't seen her for ages. I'm surprised she's here; this isn't really her thing. And I want to check in with Luke and Zack, too." She cocked her head to one side. "It was good of you to invite Angel and Maria to come tonight. This last show's a big deal to you, isn't it?"

He dropped a kiss on her lips. "It's huge. I told you. I'm hoping it's going to be the best night of my life."

"Have you got something going on that I don't know about? You're not sneaking some new material into the set, are you? You know we should talk about it before you—"

He put a finger over her lips. "Do you trust me?"

She nodded.

"Good. I wrote a new song. I'm going to play it."

She started to speak, but he pressed his finger on her lips to make her stop.

"If you trust me, you won't say anything until we come off stage later. Then you can tell me if it was a bad idea."

She sighed.

He gave her his best *aren't-I-adorable, how-could-you-say-no-to-me* smile. And she realized that she really couldn't say no to him. She smiled back. "Okay."

Matt looked out past the lights and into the crowd. This was it. This was his moment. The show was going great. The night couldn't be any more perfect. Thousands of fans screamed back at him when he yelled, "How are you doing, Seattle?"

He grinned at Lance as he pulled his guitar strap over his head and went to set it down against the drums. West raised an eyebrow at him, and he nodded. The time had come.

West hit a drumroll and finished with a loud cymbal crash as Matt turned back to the crowd. "There's been a lot of crazy stories flying around about me over the last few months. Do you want to know the truth?"

The crowd went wild, and Matt shot a look over at the wings. Clay stood there with his arm around Autumn's shoulders. It was Clay's job to make sure she was there and didn't go disappearing. He caught her eye and chuckled when he saw her expression. She didn't like this; didn't like it one bit. She hated when he went off script.

"Okay. Well, I want to put to bed a rumor once and for all. I tried to set it straight in the press that little Evie is not my daughter. But I know there's still all kinds of crap flying around that she might be. I'll be honest with you. I hope one day I do have a daughter of my own, and if she's as sweet as Evie, I'll be one happy guy. In the meantime, I'd like you to meet her real dad." He gestured to the other side of the stage and Sean, his driver and quasi-security guy walked Richard and Yvonne—Evie's parents out onto the stage. Matt hugged them both. Then he spoke into the mic again. "These guys have been through a lot because of me—and they don't deserve it. I asked them here tonight for a few reasons. I want to ask you all to show them your love—and to give them a break from now on."

Richard and Yvonne smiled at him gratefully as the stadium erupted in thunderous applause.

"Thanks, everyone." He smiled. "That was only part of the reason that they're here. See, they know who the real woman in my life is. I met them here in Seattle a few months ago—on the same weekend that I finally started to persuade my best friend that she's so much more than a friend to me."

The last of the applause died away, and the whole place went still and silent.

Matt grinned. "Do you want to know who she is?"

The response was deafening. He waved them to be quiet again. "Okay. I don't have a little girl, but I want you to meet the woman I call my baby girl." He turned and held his hand out to Autumn. She looked madder than a wet cat and shook her head at him rapidly.

"Damn," he grinned at the crowd. "I might be blowing this here. Want to help me out?"

"Let's help him out," Levi spoke into his mic. "Come on, everyone. Let's get her out here." He, too, turned to look at Autumn and started up a chant. "Come on out. Come on out."

Matt couldn't help but laugh. He hadn't planned for what he might do if she refused, but thanks to Levi and the crowd, she really didn't have a choice.

Clay planted a kiss on the top of her head and gave her a little push. She took a few steps and then looked back.

"Here she comes," said Matt.

The chanting died down and turned to absolute silence as the crowd recognized who it was.

Matt held his arm out to her, and she came to stand beside him. She did not look happy. He couldn't help it. He dropped a kiss on her lips and murmured, "Sorry, baby girl, I had to." He looked out into the crowd. "We were going to tell you about us a whole lot sooner than this, but we decided that we wanted to keep our love to ourselves for a while."

Autumn scowled at him. They'd agreed that they shouldn't go public until the tour was over. She'd been okay with their friends knowing, but she'd still been cautious. Matt had wanted to give her all the time she needed, but now the tour was almost over, and he'd waited as long as he could.

"Now, though, I want to share it with you. And I want to share the most important moment of my life with you guys. You know I love you all. I know my life wouldn't be what it is without you. I know it, and I appreciate each and every one of you. But none of you would ever even have heard my name if it wasn't for this beautiful woman right here. She's made me the man I am in every sense. Going forward, my life can't be what I want it to be until I do this." He turned back to Autumn and dropped a kiss on her startled lips before he went down on one knee.

~ ~ ~

Autumn stared down at him as he held onto her hand and dug in his pocket. She couldn't believe this was happening. Her heart was racing. Whenever she'd been out on stage before, she'd hated it. She didn't like all those people watching her. Now, she loved it. She got it. She could feel the love from them, just like Matt talked about so often. They didn't feel like a huge intrusive presence, they faded away to just a warm feeling, which still couldn't compare with the love she felt and saw shining in Matt's eyes. He squeezed her hand.

"Baby girl."

She nodded.

"You are the best thing that's ever happened to me. I've wanted to be your man since the first day we met. You kicked my tour into shape. Then you kicked my career into shape." He smiled and glanced out at the crowd. "And I have to tell you, she's kicked my ass into shape and made me the man I am today." He looked back at her. "I love you with all my heart and soul, Autumn. I promise you I'll love you for the rest of my days. Please say you'll walk through life by my side. Please say you'll be my wife. Let me love you and do my best to make you happy till the day I die."

She stared down into his eyes, and tears pricked behind her own as she nodded. She couldn't think of anything she wanted more in life than to spend it with him. "Yes."

He slid a ring onto her finger and stood up to close his arms around her as the crowd went wild. "I love you, baby girl."

"I love you, too."

"I'll do everything I can to make you happy."

She smiled. "Does that include never springing a surprise like this on me again?"

His smile disappeared. "I'm sorry. I thought ... I ..."

She pecked his lips. "It's okay. It's wonderful. It's right." She looked out at the crowd who was still screaming and clapping. "This is a huge part of our life. This is how it should be."

He lowered his lips to kiss her, and the noise and the bright lights faded away as she got lost in the feel of him.

When they finally came up for air, he grinned at the crowd. "She said yes!"

Lance came out with a stool, and she perched on it while Matt got his guitar. "I wrote this one, especially for this moment. It's called 'Baby Girl'."

When the show was over and he came off stage, he came straight to her. She watched him, loving the thought that he was now her fiancé—her future husband. He slid his arms around her and hugged her tight to his chest. "I'm sorry I sprang it on you like that—out there. But …"

She planted a kiss on his lips. "It's okay. It was right. That was how it should be."

Everyone started to crowd around them, congratulating them. They got lost in a sea of hugs and handshakes. Everyone wanted to talk to them.

Clay hugged them both and told them how proud he was of them. Autumn understood now why Matt had invited seemingly everyone they knew, and she was glad of it. She hadn't been expecting this to be the most important night of her life so far, but she was happy that they got to share it with their friends and family.

She smiled to herself as Summer and Carter came to them. Summer hugged Matt tight. "Who would have thought when we first toured together all those years ago, that you'd end up being my brother-in-law?"

He grinned at her. "I didn't even dare dream it."

"It didn't occur to me back then, but I've been waiting for this day for a long time." Summer smiled at Autumn, and Autumn made a face back at her. She knew what was coming.

Summer smiled sweetly. "I asked you a long time ago if I had permission to say it when this day came."

Autumn couldn't help but smile. "And I only agreed that you could because I never thought it would happen."

"You didn't think what would happen?" asked Matt. "What do you need to say?"

Summer hugged her and then stood back with a triumphant look on her face. "I told my sister here, years ago that you two would end up together, and when you did, I would get to say—I told you so!"

Matt laughed. He knew how much Autumn hated to hear those words. He put his arm around her shoulders and looked down at her. "I'll bet that hurts."

She planted a kiss on his lips. "Not one bit. For once in my life, I can honestly say that I couldn't be happier that Summer was right, or that I was wrong." She laughed as he exchanged an incredulous glance with Summer.

"Can I get that in writing?" he asked.

"Nope, and you may never hear me say those three words again."

"I can live without hearing you say *I was wrong*, as long as you never stop saying *I love you*."

She smiled. "I plan to tell you that one every day for the rest of my life."

She was vaguely aware of Summer and Carter walking away when Matt kissed her; vaguely, but all she really knew was the feel of his arms around her and his lips on hers.

It felt like hours went by with everyone wanting a word, wanting to talk and congratulate them. When Matt got her to himself for a moment, he kissed her neck and whispered into her ear. "I thought when I came off stage we'd be done, and we'd have each other to ourselves."

She smiled. "You know better than that. We never get to be by ourselves until late at night."

He smiled and eyed her breasts. "Bring on the night."

;

A Note from SJ

I hope you enjoyed Autumn and Matt's story. Please let your friends know about the books if you feel they would enjoy them as well. It would be wonderful if you would leave me a review; I'd very much appreciate it.

There are so many more stories still to tell. I hope you enjoyed getting to know the rest of the band I'm sure you can see a few more couples vying for position in this Nashville series. I'm excited to get to them. They're going to have to wait a while though. The next book I'll have ready for you will be the next Summer Lake Silver story. I'm so glad I finally get to write Seymour and Chris's story. (he's Hope Davenport's father from the A Chance and a Hope series, and she is Jack and Dan's mum from the original Summer Lake series. I plan to release their book on August 24th.

I do have a plan for the rest of this year – there'll be another Summer Lake Seasons story and the next in the Nashville series. Plans can and do change -especially with me, so if you want to keep up with the latest news on which books to expect next, and other snippets of my writing world, be sure to sign up for my newsletter. You'll be in the loop for giveaways and sneak peeks that way, too.

In the meantime, check out the "Also By" page to see if any of my other series appeal to you – I have a couple of freebie series starters, too, so you can take them for a test drive.

There are a few options to keep up with me and my imaginary friends:

The best way is to Sign up for my Newsletter at my website www.SJMcCoy.com. Don't worry I won't bombard you! I'll let you know about upcoming releases, share a sneak peek or two and keep you in the loop for a couple of fun giveaways I have coming up :0)

You can join my readers group to chat about the books or like my Facebook Page www.facebook.com/authorsjmccoy

I occasionally attempt to say something in 140 characters or less(!) on Twitter

And I'm in the process of building a shiny new website at www.SJMcCoy.com

I love to hear from readers, so feel free to email me at SJ@SJMcCoy.com if you'd like. I'm better at that! :0)

I hope our paths will cross again soon. Until then, take care, and thanks for your support—you are the reason I write!

Love

SJ

PS Project Semicolon

You may have noticed that the final sentence of the story closed with a semi-colon. It isn't a typo. Project Semi Colon is a non-profit movement dedicated to presenting hope and love to those who are struggling with depression, suicide, addiction and self-injury. Project Semicolon exists to encourage, love and inspire. It's a movement I support with all my heart.

"A semicolon represents a sentence the author could have ended, but chose not to. The sentence is your life and the author is you." - Project Semicolon

This author started writing after her son was killed in a car crash. At the time I wanted my own story to be over, instead I chose to honour a promise to my son to write my 'silly stories' someday. I chose to escape into my fictional world. I know for many who struggle with depression, suicide can appear to be the only escape. The semicolon has become a symbol of support, and hopefully a reminder – Your story isn't over yet

Also by SJ McCoy

Summer Lake Seasons
Angel and Luke in Take These Broken Wings
Zack and Maria in Too Much Love to Hide

Summer Lake Silver
Clay and Marianne in Like Some Old Country Song

Summer Lake Series
Love Like You've Never Been Hurt (FREE in ebook form)
Work Like You Don't Need the Money
Dance Like Nobody's Watching
Fly Like You've Never Been Grounded
Laugh Like You've Never Cried
Sing Like Nobody's Listening
Smile Like You Mean It
The Wedding Dance
Chasing Tomorrow
Dream Like Nothing's Impossible
Ride Like You've Never Fallen
Live Like There's No Tomorrow
The Wedding Flight

Remington Ranch Series
Mason (FREE in ebook form) and also available as Audio
Shane
Carter
Beau
Four Weddings and a Vendetta

A Chance and a Hope
Chance is a guy with a whole lot of story to tell. He's part of the fabric of both Summer Lake and Remington Ranch. He needed three whole books to tell his own story.

Chance Encounter
Finding Hope
Give Hope a Chance

The Davenports
Oscar
TJ
Reid

The Hamiltons
Cameron and Piper in Red wine and Roses
Chelsea and Grant in Champagne and Daisies
Mary Ellen and Antonio in Marsala and Magnolias
Marcos and Molly in Prosecco and Peonies
Coming Next
Grady

About the Author

I'm SJ, a coffee addict, lover of chocolate and drinker of good red wines. I'm a lost soul and a hopeless romantic. Reading and writing are necessary parts of who I am. Though perhaps not as necessary as coffee! I can drink coffee without writing, but I can't write without coffee.

I grew up loving romance novels, my first boyfriends were book boyfriends, but life intervened, as it tends to do, and I wandered down the paths of non-fiction for many years. My life changed completely a few years ago and I returned to Romance to find my escape.

I write 'Sweet n Steamy' stories because to me there is enough angst and darkness in real life. My favorite romances are happy escapes with a focus on fun, friendships and happily-ever-afters, just like the ones I write.

These days I live in beautiful Montana, the last best place. If I'm not reading or writing, you'll find me just down the road in the park - Yellowstone. I have deer, eagles and the occasional bear for company, and I like it that way :0)